FAIR WARNING

Catherine Sellers

A KISMET® Romance

METEOR PUBLISHING CORPORATION
Bensalem, Pennsylvania

For my dear, sweet, wonderful, kind, patient, talented, sometimes argumentative friends and fellow Condors—Rebecca Blanchard, Lisbeth Chance, Keith Cockrell, Judith Linsley, and Ellen Rienstra—for the countless hours of critiquing and for the love and support. You are the best.

With a special thank you to Sheriff Mike Holzapfel, Hardin County, Texas, and his secretary, Nancy Hazlewood.

And, as always, for Bill. . . .

CATHERINE SELLERS

According to Catherine Sellers, the definition of writing could be "a little talent and a lot of hard work combined with massive doses of frustration and self-doubt." Hardly a day goes by that she doesn't ask why she puts herself through so much turmoil. Then, on a day when nothing seems to go "write," she hears from a reader who says how much one of her stories touched her, and all the hard work, frustration, and self-doubt don't seem so overpowering. "Corresponding with readers is a pleasure," she says and invites you to write to her at: P.O. Box 8231, Lumberton, Texas 77711-0231.

Other books by Catherine Sellers:

ONE

Kendall Jamison was far too nervous to take the seat the deputy offered before he left her alone in the semi-cluttered office. She stood just inside the door, taking in her surroundings. Every piece of furniture was either slick brown vinyl or wood and sadly out of date. Even the wooden file cabinets had to be at least forty years old. The lingering odor of pungent cleaning chemicals barely masked the musty smell of old papers and even older furnishings. Bookshelves behind the not-quite antique desk overflowed with law enforcement books and procedural manuals.

Centered along the front edge of the desk was a nameplate that flashed at her like a neon sign: JACOB H. SENTELL, SMITHBORO COUNTY SHERIFF. A framed photograph stood on one corner of the desk, and she picked it up for a closer look. Nice family, she thought, her eyes moving from one small boy to the next—three of them—then to the young man who couldn't have been more than sixteen. Sitting dead center of the boys was a lovely blonde, probably in her mid-thirties, who was also very much pregnant. Beside her, smiling down, stood a tall man wearing jeans and a crisply starched white western shirt. Kendall's gaze stopped on his face. The resemblance between the all-male brood and the man was striking, but it was the look passing between husband and wife that made her heart ache. That they adored each other was as evident as the happiness reflected in each child's face.

Something akin to envy flared briefly inside her, briefly because she had vowed years ago that her emotions would never again make her vulnerable. Quickly tucking the unexpected memories back where she kept them neatly buried, she put the photo back where she'd found it.

The door behind her opened and she turned around to see the man from the photo close the door, then hang his western hat and holster and service revolver on the coatrack. She couldn't help noticing that his khaki uniform blended nicely with all the brown vinyl and wooden furniture.

"Sorry I kept you waiting," he said by way of an apology. She also couldn't help seeing that he paid her hardly any notice as he skirted his desk and took his seat. The same couldn't be said of her, though. In those few short seconds, she noticed everything about him, from the top of his dark head to the shine on his western boots.

He picked up the file that had her name neatly typed on the index tab. "Got tied up in court," he explained with an absent tug at his shirt collar as he scanned the contents of the folder that summed up her twenty-nine years in this world.

Years of habit kept her from taking the chair sitting opposite him until she was told to do so. "That's okay. If there's one thing I have plenty of, it's time."

He raised his head and looked at her. At first glance, his eyes appeared to be a shade of darkest blue, but upon closer inspection their color reminded her of smoke rising off a fire laid with wet wood. Dark charcoal gray and smoldering. His forehead furrowed, pulling his dark eyebrows together beneath the widow's peak that lent so much character to his better-than-average features. She couldn't remember the last time a man had given her such a penetrating once-over. Of course, where she'd been for the last five years, men had been few and far between.

At long last he spoke. "You don't look much like a housekeeper and nanny," he said without so much as a hint of a smile. If his expression was any indication, the man took his interviewing seriously.

Kendall'd had enough serious to last her a lifetime. "I don't look much like an ex-con either," she countered, chancing a smile that drew nothing but silence for one long, awkward moment.

Just as she was thinking she'd made a terrible mistake, he grinned back at her, "Touché. Why don't you take a load off?" He nodded toward the chair.

Relieved that she hadn't blown it, she sat down. "I was told this program was your brainchild." Maybe small talk would make her less nervous. Besides, they'd get around to talking about her soon enough.

"Yeah," he muttered, still mulling over her file. "Newly released cons need all the help they can get reentering society. Being able to find work usually decides whether or not they make it on the outside. So far our success rate's been pretty good, but there's been talk—" He cut himself off, leaving Kendall with the distinct impression he'd almost revealed too much.

"Now," he said, breaking into her thoughts and flipping the pages. "Let's see about Kendall Leigh Jamison,'' he read her full name out loud. "Nice name, but an awful picture," he added absently, and Kendall realized that he was talking to himself. "Sex: Female. Definitely. Age: Twenty-nine. Looks younger. Height: Five-ten. Weight: . . ." He looked up again. "You've put on a pound or two."

Where some might have found his self-expository comments annoying, she found them refreshing. She liked people who said what was on their minds. You knew where you stood with them. And she couldn't take offense at his observation. She had put on weight. Intentionally.

"I was slender for my height when I went in. Had to do something to protect myself, so I hit the weights. Now that I'm out, I'll lighten up."

"Looks good from where I sit," he said as a matter of fact. Then, obviously realizing how it sounded, he turned his attention back to her file. "Next of kin: None. Never been married. Served five years at Gatesville's Unit for Women for fraud." This time when he looked at her, she knew she would be answering some questions. "Want to tell me about it?"

The self-protective shield Kendall had developed in Gatesville shot up as if someone had just pressed the activate button. "There's nothing to tell. I was charged, tried, and convicted. Now, I've served my time and want to get on with my life."

His gaze seemed to take in every detail of her face at once. "Charged, tried, and convicted doesn't always add up to guilty."

Kendall felt the need to swallow. This was the last thing she'd expected a lawman to say. Not only was he nice to look at, but he seemed to possess uncanny instincts.

"Five years is kind of steep for fraud. A probated

sentence of much less than that would have been more like it.''

Kendall wasn't surprised by his comment any more than she'd been surprised the day her sentence was handed down. "It was an election year, and my case was getting a lot of publicity. The district attorney was trying to look good for the media and win brownie points with the voters.''

The sheriff simply nodded, his gesture saying he'd heard that particular story before. "Says here that you were partners with one Ellis Trammell and . . .'' He ran the index finger of his left hand down the sheet of paper in front of him, making it impossible for Kendall to miss the gold band on his ring finger. ". . . Courtney Blankenship.'' He looked her squarely in the eye. "They were never brought up on charges. Care to explain that?''

No, she didn't care to explain anything. But neither did she want to blow this interview. This job meant the difference between being forced to take just any old job and doing what she loved—working with children. "What can I say? They were just smarter and got away.''

The sheriff didn't look convinced. She knew he was thinking things over and almost wished he'd lambast her with more questions instead of sitting there studying her with those smoldering gray eyes. She felt her facade of cool indifference slip a notch.

"You don't strike me as someone who would take the rap for someone else,'' he finally said. "Unless they were important to you.''

Important? Yes, she thought, *a sister could be considered important. So could a fiancé.* "I don't see what any of this has to do with my qualifications to be someone's housekeeper and nanny. My parole officer said you knew a family who needed domestic help.'' Somewhere deep inside her, panic started to creep in. She couldn't just sit there and let this job slip away. It was time for the hard sell.

"Children are my specialty," she said. "In Houston I worked at Wee Care Day Care and took night classes to earn my degrees in psychology and early childhood development." Again she thought of the years of education and hard work down the drain because she hadn't seen past Ellis's soap-opera good looks and charm.

The sheriff must have sensed her distress because he glanced up, his face as unreadable as the thoughts running through his mind.

"But then, you already know all that, don't you?" She wasn't naive enough to think she'd gotten this far without having been thoroughly screened.

She wanted to scream at him when he nonchalantly glanced back down at her file and asked, "That about the time you got hooked up with Trammell?"

So they were back to that. "Yes, I guess it was." She'd have to be careful here. "He was a promoter looking for help to get his Little Miss Houston Pageant organized. He needed people experienced in dealing with children. Courtney and I were looking for ways to earn extra money, and he hired us both on the spot."

"So you knew Blankenship before you met Trammell?"

The man was sharp. She'd been so intent on downplaying her relationship with Ellis that she'd let that slip. Still, she was okay. Because of the different last names, no one ever made the connection between Kendall and her stepsister—and legally they weren't even that. And that was the way Kendall wanted to keep it.

Nonetheless, she wasn't one to out and out lie about anything—unless it was to protect Courtney. Which Kendall still found hard to understand. When Courtney hadn't come back on her own to clear her, Kendall hadn't said anything to implicate Courtney. In her head she knew that the baby Courtney was carrying had to be the reason Courtney had let her take the fall. Her heart, however, ached from the betrayal she felt, not only because Courtney had deserted her, but also because Courtney had obviously been seeing Ellis behind her back.

After she was sentenced and started to serve her time, the hurt turned into anger. As time went on, she became bitter. Disillusioned, she swore never to allow Courtney back into her life to cause her more grief. Now that the damage had been done, it made no sense to do anything but play it out to the end.

"Well, yes. She and I took some classes together." This much, at least, was true, but if she weren't careful, this man would pick information out of her piece by piece. "Like I said, what does any of this have to do with my—"

"Relax." He placed the file on the desk and leaned forward. "Is there anything you think you should tell me up front?"

Kendall knew the sheriff was fishing. Just as she knew he was giving her a chance most people wouldn't give a jailbird. Still, there was no way he could know about Courtney's postcards. They'd started coming shortly after she'd settled in at Gatesville, and, in spite of her vow never to see Courtney again, she'd read and saved each one. Besides, she'd signed each of them Corky, her nickname, and had never used a return address. Kendall's only clue to her sister's whereabouts had been the postmarks. And there had been dozens of them over the years, the last being New Orleans, which was over five hundred miles southeast of Rosemont.

Pointedly, Kendall looked at the file lying open in

front of the sheriff, then met his gaze with a steady one of her own. "My life's an open book."

Sheriff Sentell glanced down at the file, then back at her. "So that's how you want to play it?" His voice, though soft, held a resigned edge, and that made Kendall uneasy. "Okay. Your file looks good. You were a model prisoner. Is there anything you want to know about the job?"

Kendall breathed easier. Apparently he was going to let it slide. "Yes, of course. First, how many children are we talking about?"

"Four. Three boys, ages ten, thirteen, and fifteen, who are in school all day. And a girl, almost three, who'll demand most of your time."

"And the housekeeping duties. Exactly what will I be expected to do?"

"Everything. Tend the house, cook, wash clothes, take the boys to and from ball practice. You know, mother stuff."

"I take it that the mother is . . . ?"

"Dead."

Couldn't get any plainer than that.

"And the father?"

"Is too busy to take care of things the way he should. The present housekeeper has been with the family since . . . a few months before the little girl's birth, but she has to leave in less than a week to take care of an aging mother in Alabama. Did I mention that room and board are part of the salary?"

"No. But my P.O. did. She explained that the father works long, sometimes unusual hours and that it would be a live-in situation. Which suits me fine." She didn't relish the chore of trying to find an apartment in a new town. Especially one so small that curiosity and questions were inevitable. All she wanted was to settle in and get on with her new life. No fuss. No muss. No hassle.

"Then you're still at the halfway house?"

"Yes. It's not ideal, but it beats the streets."

"Not anymore. Starting tonight, you'll be moving—"

"Wait a minute. Doesn't the man I'll be working for have to okay this? Besides, I might want to ask *him* a few questions." Ex-con though she might be, she had every intention of exercising her rights as a free, law-abiding citizen. What if she didn't like him, or vice versa? Or worse—what if he turned out to be a fanny-pinching lecher?

"Fine." The sheriff leaned back in his squeaky desk chair. "Fire away."

All Kendall seemed capable of was blinking her eyes at him. "You?" She glanced at the photograph on his desk, then back at him. "But—"

"It's an old picture." He leaned forward again and pointed to the oldest of the boys. "That's Brad. He's away at college now. University of Texas," he said with pride. He moved his finger to each of the other boys. "Joshua. Timothy. Matthew." Kendall didn't miss the way his eyes lingered on the woman or the flicker of pain that registered briefly on his face. "And . . ." He turned to a photo sitting on the credenza behind him. A dark-haired, green-eyed enchantress of about three smiled back at him. "This is Becca." The impish little face should have lessened the pain Kendall saw reflected in his eyes, but it didn't.

"That's a houseful of kids," she said, hoping to put a smile back on his face.

It worked. "Tell me about it. Now, you said you had a few questions for me. Shoot."

Momentarily stunned, she forgot every question she'd rehearsed this morning in the bathroom mirror.

All she wanted to know at the moment was how his wife had died. Knowing it would be rude to ask something so personal, she searched her memory for the pertinent list of questions.

"All right. Do you have a backup for my days off or in case I get sick and can't work?"

"I think I can arrange something. My sister-in-law and her housekeeper have filled in for Esther from time to time."

"Will I have to do the shopping? You know, for groceries, clothes for the kids, that kind of thing?"

"McElvey's Grocery delivers once a week. All you have to do is call in your order or drop off a list a day in advance. As for the other, only if you're comfortable doing so."

"Then you have no objections to my taking your children with me—"

"Miss Jamison," he cut in. "Although the owners of Wee Care Day Care regretted not being able to offer you your old job, they remembered you fondly and gave you a glowing recommendation." That statement reminded her of the repercussions of her decision to protect Courtney. She'd lost so much. Five years of her life, her reputation, her dream to one day own and operate her own day care center. She didn't doubt for a moment that Kacy and Mary hated not being able to hire her back, but she also knew that they had a growing business to protect. Many of Wee Care's parents hadn't been happy to learn that two of the workers who spent so much time with their children had been involved in the scam that stirred up so much publicity.

"You will run my home as if it were your own," she heard the sheriff saying. "All I ask is that you consult with me on certain matters, keep me informed on what's going on with my boys at school and their various outside interests. I try to keep up, but sometimes it just isn't possible. Anything else?''

From the moment she realized she'd be living in the same house with a single man, she'd known she would have to set some ground rules of her own. Nothing had changed just because the man in question was the sheriff.

"Yes." She straightened in her chair. "I want it clearly understood that this is to be a working relationship only, Sheriff. I watch your children, clean your house, cook your meals. That's where my duties stop.''

One dark eyebrow shot up, then lowered, as did his tone of voice. "If I can trust you with my children, I think you can trust me with you.''

That certainly put her in her place, she thought, beginning to squirm under his intense scrutiny.

"There's one other thing we need to get settled, Miss Jamison." His tone was even more somber now. "There are times when peace officers have to give suspects a warning shot. I feel it only fair that I do the same with you. Since you have no family, people from your past are expressly forbidden to associate with my children.''

"So you're giving me fair warning." Always one to respond honestly, Kendall squared her shoulders defensively. "If you don't want me working for you, Sheriff, just say so.''

"It's not that, I assure you.''

"Then what?''

"I see you like everything laid out nice and neat. Good. So do I." He swiveled around to face her squarely. "As you already know, this program is my baby. And, as I told you, our success rate has been better than any of us ever dreamed it would be. However, our few failures were nothing short of disasters and our funding is in jeopardy. We need that money. What better way to convince the people controlling the purse strings how much I believe in this program—"

"Than to hire an ex-con to take care of your family."

Jacob Sentell's expression was a study in control. "Good. We understand each other. I don't want anyone from your past—Trammell or Blankenship in particular—showing up to cause trouble. Now," he said, coming to his feet, "if we're in agreement, I'll give you directions—"

"Sorry," Kendall interrupted. "I don't own a car. I took the bus from Houston to Rosemont, and at the moment I find myself financially embarrassed. Taxi fare would really put me in the red."

"No problem." He obviously took setbacks in stride. "If you'll wait outside, I'll finish up a few things here, then drive you to the halfway house to pick up your things. I'd like you to meet Esther before the boys get home. It gets kind of hectic around four o'clock."

Kendall was on her feet by the time he reached the door and opened it for her. "Sheriff." He turned to look at her. "I may have misled you about one little thing . . ."

Again, his forehead furrowed. "And what might that be?"

"Well," she said, trying not to smile. "I used to be a fair to middling cook, but it's been a while since I stood in front of a stove." She saw *him* trying not to smile back.

"I think we can work around that."

Jake Sentell sat in his patrol car, watching Kendall Jamison mount the steps to the halfway house, then disappear inside. The crisp March air felt good on his skin and he leaned across the seat to lower the passenger's window so the breeze could blow through. The azaleas and dogwoods were in full bloom and the air was sweet with honeysuckle and budding roses. Old neighborhoods. He loved them, but this morning his attention wasn't on anything except the woman who would be sleeping under the same roof with him. Which brought his thoughts back to what he hoped wouldn't be a problem later on.

He'd started having doubts about hiring her from the moment he glanced up over her file to see her studying him so closely with those bluer-than-blue eyes. Of course he'd known all about her from her file, and mug shots were notorious for being unflattering. Still, the woman in the photo, who looked almost anorexic, with dark circles under each eye and stringy hair that fell limply around her gaunt features, was a far cry from the vibrant, vital young woman he had just interviewed.

He'd begun interviewing for the position the day after Esther gave him her notice. His search had been difficult from the start. Not just any ex-con would do where his children were concerned. He'd found flaw after flaw with each applicant and was beginning to think he'd have to abandon his plan to recruit someone from the reentry program he'd started two years ago. Then Kendall Leigh Jamison's file arrived from her parole officer in Houston.

On paper she was perfect, exactly what he was looking for. She had a background of working with children, wanted to move to a smaller town, and her crime, though serious, had not been one of violence, nor had it been drug related. And, as he'd told her, she'd been a model prisoner who posed no threat to society. He'd all but made the decision to hire her from the information in her file and the references from her P.O. and ex-employers. The interview had been merely a formality.

Then he'd seen her standing by his desk and had to make a pretense of studying the file he already knew by heart. In person, she was also perfect. Tall and slender, she was dressed in form-fitting jeans, sneakers so white they had to be new, and a long-sleeved cotton shirt that matched the color of her eyes almost exactly. Her hair, he'd noticed, was a soft reddish blond and was swept away from her face and off her shoulders in one of those French braids Becca loved so much. All in all, Kendall Jamison was a striking woman with crystal clear blue eyes, a pert nose that hadn't been spared a freckle or two, and lips free of lipstick—

He chopped off the thought with a vengeance, but his subconscious mind insisted on going on with its analysis. She'd tried valiantly to mask her nervousness behind lighthearted wisecracks, but he'd seen the way she chewed on her bottom lip when she thought he wasn't watching, heard the insecurity in the way she tried to skirt some of his questions. And she'd been right about his already knowing all there was to know about her. He couldn't quite nail it down, but he suspected that she'd been less than honest with him about Blankenship. Why? From all accounts, Kendall had been the scapegoat in the baby pageant scam, the one left behind to deal with irate parents, the news media, and a consumer/business panel that was sick of scam artists hitting Harris County, Texas, and moving on with hundreds of thousands of Houston dollars in their pockets. The fact that it had been an election year, he had no doubt, had indeed earned her a harsher sentence than she'd have received under normal circumstances. And having a rookie public defender certainly hadn't helped matters. If only she had cooperated by giving the district attorney information on Trammell and Blankenship. But she hadn't said a word about her partners, had taken the heat alone.

Still, he thought, he couldn't disregard the way he'd felt seeing her standing there. Almost three years had passed since his Becky's death, and although his time of mourning was officially over, he never, *never* reacted to women the way he'd responded to this one. Unconsciously, he fingered his wedding band. He wasn't ready for a relationship, physical or otherwise, now or any time in the near future. Especially with someone who would be working for him, living in his home. And yet, he'd be a fool to let her slip away. The program was in jeopardy, and his children needed someone to care for them. God knew he hadn't been home much lately.

To make matters worse, he was pressed for time. Esther would be leaving for Alabama Saturday morning. That left only five days to get the new housekeeper settled in.

Voices calling from the house roused him from his thoughts. He glanced up to see Kendall hugging Mrs. Arnold, the halfway house matron, then wave to the others gathered on the front porch. Kendall. He smiled, liking the sound of her name. It was . . . her. Beautiful. Different. Ultrafeminine. And, he decided in a heartbeat, he couldn't trust himself to think of her in those terms. Consequently, he also decided, he would never use her given name.

She hadn't just been being nice when she'd told him not to bother with helping her, that she didn't have that much to gather up. A small canvas tote swung in one hand as she descended the steps and headed toward the curb where he waited.

Again he found himself watching her as any healthy,

red-blooded male would. Now that he was looking for it, he saw the evidence of body building she'd mentioned in his office. Even through the denim that covered her lower body, he saw the firm, well-developed upper thighs, the flat contours of her abdomen. She'd probably put on no more than ten pounds, but every ounce of it was muscle.

She slid into the front seat beside him, placing her tote between them. Immediately the interior of the patrol car was permeated with the fresh, sweet scent of soap and shampoo and Kendall Jamison.

"Well, Jamison," he said, turning the key in the ignition, "ready to meet the 'Wrecking Crew'?"

"That bad, huh?"

Jake smiled to himself, then looked at her. Sitting there without a trace of makeup, her hair pulled away from her face, she made him forget to breathe. He had a sudden image of her hair unbound, hanging free and loose around her face. He could almost feel it in his hands—

"Let's just say they can be a handful," he forced himself to say.

"I think I can hold my own. You might want to ask if they're ready for me. And speaking of me . . ." She cleared her throat. "Are we going to level with them or not?"

"Ball's in my court, right?" Jake hadn't given this much thought, but he'd never been less than honest with his children. He wouldn't be starting now. "We'll tell them like it is."

"You're the boss."

She said it without hesitation or emotion, but Jake heard the fear lurking just beneath her resolve. For all her outward confidence, she was scared to death.

TWO

They pulled away from the curb and headed down the shady, oak-lined street Kendall had strolled along every day since arriving in Rosemont last Friday afternoon, two full days before this morning's interview with the sheriff. The idea of being cooped up in her room all weekend hadn't appealed to her in the least. That all the doors locked from the inside and she could come and go at will hadn't mattered. She'd spent the better part of the next two days simply taking in the sights of what she soon learned was the Old Town District. What she'd told the sheriff was true; she didn't have a spare dime to her name. Thankfully, the walking tour had cost her nothing more than some leg work and a little time.

Markers all over told of the small town's colorful history. The bricks used to lay the streets downtown around the turn of the century had come from Rosemont's own brick plant, she learned, and the old train depot, once the center for trade and commerce, now housed an oil field museum. But her favorite find had been the Dixieland Hotel Museum.

Late Saturday afternoon, she'd been standing on the front gallery of the three-story Greek Revival structure, reading the plaque that related the Dixieland's history and recent renovation, when the door opened and the curator greeted her. Had her financial situation not been so dire, she'd gladly have paid the five-dollar admission fee for the tour.

She needn't have worried, though. Mrs. Resnick, a slender woman in her early fifties, proved to be a delight, and the conversation she struck up ended with an invitation for afternoon tea.

Two hours later Kendall had been given the grand tour of the notorious old bawdyhouse that during its heyday had been nothing more than an embarrassment, but today was one of the town's most popular claims to fame.

Kendall smiled, remembering the walk home later that evening with the fresh March wind on her face. The panorama of color effected by blooming azaleas and dogwoods and wisteria was as delightful as the fragrant mixture of freshly mowed grass and honeysuckle.

But today another scent, one that was as pleasant as it was unnerving, assailed her senses. That of Jacob Sentell's after-shave.

Beside her he drove in silence, and Kendall sensed a change in his demeanor that, frankly, had her puzzled. Not even the sight of bridal wreath blooming in a profusion of frothy white in the center median could distract her from his solemn expression. She hadn't given it much thought earlier when he'd called her Jamison. At Gatesville last names were the rule rather than the exception, but something in the way he said it left her with the impression that he'd done so with premeditation. Why was anyone's guess, but now, with the silence stretching between them like the miles between the halfway house and the city limits sign, she had to wonder at his reasons for not using her given name or, at the very least, *Miss* Jamison.

"Is something wrong?" she asked, her penchant for getting to the point surprising even her.

He turned his attention from driving to look at her. "Why do you ask?"

She hated it when someone answered a question with a question. Two could play that game. "Why don't you just answer me?" His profile was to her again, and she saw the muscle beneath his sideburn begin to work.

"I was thinking about what you said about keeping our relationship on an employer/employee basis." He paused, seeming to choose his words carefully. "That might prove easier said than done. I hadn't counted on your being so . . . so . . ." Obviously her trait of being open was one they shared. He reached up and took his hat off, then placed it on the seat between them. Both windows were down, and the wind whipped his dark, wavy hair about his face.

"Young and attractive?" No one had ever accused Kendall of being conceited or vain. It was just that she had eyes in her head and the mirror didn't lie.

"I like your straightforwardness," he answered with a wry little grin. "Yeah. Young and attractive never occurred to me the whole time I was looking for someone to take Esther's place. Your mug shot wasn't very flattering," he said with a laugh. "Could present a whole passel of new problems," he went on to say, more to himself than to her, she suspected.

And she wasn't offended by his observation; somehow it never entered her mind that he might be giving himself too much credit in the appeal department. As attractive as he was, he didn't come across any more egotistical than she did.

"Sheriff, I may not have . . ." She stopped. How could she put this delicately? Honest to a fault about most things, she was the one having to stop and think now. "Granted, my love life's been on hold for five years, but I think I can control my libidinal instincts." She really didn't enjoy shocking people, but some things simply had to be spelled out. "If that's what's bothering you," she finished with the straightest face she could muster.

Again he smiled. "That about covers it." He didn't get a chance to say more because they left the four-lane highway that had taken them out of town and turned onto an unpaved country lane. Outside her window, she saw acre after acre of rose fields, and, in the sideview mirror, she could see the red clay kicking up, leaving a dusty trail in their wake.

"The house is just around this bend." The sheriff turned the car into a gravel driveway that led to a picture-book house situated well off the road. She read the sign hanging over the gate that read: WELCOME TO COLD CREEK RANCH & ROSE FARM—A SUBSIDIARY OF SENTELL ENTERPRISES.

At first glance the impression was surreal. But the closer they got, the more picturesque it all appeared. In the middle of a pasture and encompassed by a wooden fence, stood a two-story farmhouse, complete with a wraparound veranda on both the ground and second floors. White trim tidied up the pastel yellow paint job of an abode that was as old as it was large and charming. Vibrant yellow jonquils lined the walkway that led from the circular drive to the front steps, while yellow and red pansies encircled each of the two live oaks in the yard.

As she took in every detail of the neatly manicured lawn, with its rosebushes and azaleas and other blooming foliage, an older woman appeared on the wide front gallery. Waving, she wiped her hands on her apron and started down the steps to meet them as the car came to a stop.

"You made good time," she said to the sheriff, who hauled Kendall's bag out on his side of the patrol car.

"Traffic was light," he answered. "Esther, this is Kendall Jamison, the woman I've hired to help out after you're gone. Jamison, this is Esther O'Malley."

Kendall wasn't sure what she'd been expecting, but it wasn't a big hug and an arm around her waist to usher her inside the house.

"I'm so glad Jake found you. We were beginning to worry." She stepped back and gave Kendall a thorough once-over. "Goodness, you're a healthy specimen." She laughed, a good-natured laugh that put Kendall at ease. "You don't know how handy that's going to be." She and Jake exchanged smiles.

"Where do you want me to put this, Esther?" he asked, holding up Kendall's tote.

"Well, I'm in the middle of packing my things, so I guess you'll have to put them in the guest room."

Kendall saw Jake's expression tighten, then relax when Esther said, "Would you mind looking in on Becca while you're upstairs? She had an early lunch and is already down for her nap. If I'd known sooner that you'd be home, I'd have kept her up for you."

"That's okay. If nothing unexpected comes up, I'll try to be home early tonight. I'll see her then," Jake called over his shoulder as he took the stairs two at a time.

"Goodness, child, is that all the luggage you have?" Esther asked, herding Kendall down the spic-and-span entry hall and toward the back of the house.

Kendall loved the sound of their footfalls on the

gleaming hardwood floors. "Afraid so." She wasn't sure how much the sheriff had told his housekeeper about her past, but she was prepared for any questions the conspicuous absence of luggage might provoke.

Thankfully, Esther wasn't one to poke around in others' business. "I see," she answered instead, gesturing for Kendall to be seated at the table that had been set for two. "Lunch is ready when you and Jake are. I hope a fresh chef salad's all right. I didn't have much time after Jake called to say he was bringing you home."

Home. Kendall liked the sound of it. Ever since Momma died, home had been a place for others, never for her. But here, in this house, it felt as though she belonged. Suddenly, with the superstition of a child, she pushed the thought away. If she wanted it, even thought about it, something would happen to destroy it.

"A salad's perfect, but you shouldn't have—"

"Now, don't be telling me I shouldn't have bothered. Taking care of folks is what I do best." Esther positively beamed with pride as she placed two salad plates and glasses of iced tea on the table. "I have pecan pie for dessert. It's been cooling for an hour or so. Should still be warm." She looked Kendall over again, and her forehead wrinkled above her wire-rimmed glasses. "I hope you're not one of those health nuts who won't eat anything but wheat germ, sprouts, and bran."

Kendall laughed. "I'd love some pie." She wouldn't have refused this woman anything. "I'm not as much of a health nut as you might think. I just like keeping fit." That seemed to please the older woman, who was still fussing with the table by the time Jake appeared in the doorway. She saw by his expression that he hadn't expected to stay for lunch. Still, he sat in the chair at the head of the table like an obedient and respectful son might have.

"Looks great, Esther," he said, adding a liberal dose of Italian dressing to his salad. "Becca's sleeping like an angel." He took a bite or two while Esther hovered over them, making sure neither wanted for anything.

"Jamison here tells me that her cooking skills are sort of rusty," Jake said several minutes later. "Would you mind giving her a refresher course before you leave?" he asked with a smile no woman could resist.

Again Esther beamed. "I'll go get my cookbook out of my suitcase right this minute. We'll go over a few of the family's favorite recipes before the boys get home."

Kendall likened the stillness that followed in Esther's wake to the calm following a storm. "Is she always this energetic?"

"Chasing Becca around all day and keeping up with three active boys keeps her spry, or so she says." He stood, the sound of his chair scraping across the hardwood floor signaling his impending departure. "Think I'll pass on the pie," he called to Esther. "Save me a piece for supper." Then to Kendall he said, "You're in good hands. See you tonight."

By the time Esther returned with the cookbook in hand, Kendall heard the front door open and close.

"I swear that man works himself too hard." Esther's grimace bespoke her concern.

"That speaks well of him."

Now Esther looked plain worried. "Yes, child, it does. But he spends far too much time on the job and not enough—" She cut herself short, then placed the book on the table. "Why don't we let these dishes wait while I show you around the house? Once Becca's up, we won't have a minute to ourselves."

Esther started with the utility room just off the

kitchen to the back, then led Kendall back down the hardwood entry hall. "This is my room, where you'll be staying after I've gone," she said, indicating the room next to the kitchen. "The furniture is mine, so we'll have to see about getting you your own before I leave."

The room was nice, clean, and neat. Custom bedding of palest mint green complemented the country look, and a braided area rug in pastel shades accentuated the homespun mood by bringing out the mauve and mint in the floral wallpaper. Still, the thing that caught Kendall's eye was the window seat between the bathroom and the closet. Softly shirred eyelet valances added the finishing touch. Since the house faced the east, the window would never have any direct sun, which would make it the perfect place to curl up with a good book whenever she had the chance. Reading had become one of her favorite pastimes over the years.

"Next we have Jake's study." Esther interrupted her thoughts by sliding open a set of heavy pocket doors. In contrast to Esther's room, this one was dark and overpowering. Its only saving grace, as far as Kendall was concerned, was the French doors leading out to the front gallery. Afternoon sun filled the richly paneled room with enough light for Kendall to fully appreciate the massive mahogany desk and overstuffed leather furniture. The bookshelves behind the desk fairly overflowed with books of every kind. A stack of firewood and a smaller stack of kindling lay on the fireplace hearth. Above the mantel hung a larger copy of the family portrait she'd seen in his office in town. But unlike his office in the courthouse, the sheriff's study was dust-free and uncluttered. It was also dark and imposing, much like the man who owned the house.

"And across the hall here we have the living room."

Again, pocket doors glided open to reveal another room where each piece of furniture, she sensed, had been selected with care and the knowledge of what was both functional and pleasing to the eye.

Next was the family room, which was as large as it was cozy. A big-screen TV and entertainment center took up one entire wall and a stone fireplace presided over another. The furnishings here were less formal, chosen for comfort, and, considering the number of children in the household, its ability to take whatever a large family could dish out. Jake Sentell had an obvious taste for the good life, she thought, getting only a glimpse of the formal dining room before Esther led the way up the stairs. In the back of Kendall's mind the thought that an elected county official couldn't afford to live like this niggled at her, but she immediately pushed it away. It was none of her business how much money Jake Sentell had—or how he'd come by it.

At the top landing, Kendall saw her bag sitting on the floor in front of a closed door. Looking down the hall, she saw two more rooms on the left, three on the right, making six rooms in all, not counting the common bath at the far end.

Esther picked up Kendall's bag and opened the door. "This is the guest room."

If the rooms downstairs had been a surprise, this one was the topper. A king-size bed, lavish with custom bedding and myriad pillows, dominated one entire wall, and Queen Anne pieces complemented the various antiques placed about the room. Plush jade carpet cushioned each step while pulling together the peach, cream, and jade of the rich brocade wallpaper and the floral accents of the matching bedspread and window dressings. *Romantic boudoir* would have been Kendall's choice of words for describing what Esther kept referring to as the guest room.

"Esther," she began, hearing the surprise in her own voice. "This looks more like the master bedroom than a guest room."

Esther placed Kendall's bag on the bed, then stood back and looked around the room. "It used to be Jake and Becky's room." Kendall heard the softening in Esther's tone. "The night she died he moved his things to the room at the end of the hall. His sister-in-law Leza and I packed Becky's things shortly after that and got rid of them. I don't think he's set foot in here since."

"You were with the family when——" Kendall stopped, realizing that she was on the verge of prying.

"It's okay." Esther looked around the room. "I came to help out when Becky found out she was pregnant with Becca. She was so tired all the time, what with four rambunctious boys to take care of and all. It was more than one frail woman could handle. I'm just glad I was here at the end. They all took Becky's death hard. Especially Jake." She must have thought she'd said enough because she took a deep breath and pointed out the bathroom behind Kendall.

Automatically Kendall checked out the bathroom and dressing area, then followed the older woman back into the hall. Questions were flying around inside her head. How had Becky died? Neither the sheriff nor Esther had actually said. That an entire family had grieved so deeply touched Kendall beyond description. No one, other than her mother, had ever loved her like that. She hadn't seen her father since the day he deserted them when she was ten, and since Momma had died seven years before the trouble in Houston, there had been no one in the courtroom for moral support. What got to

Kendall most of all was knowing how hurt the sheriff had been by the death of his wife. He tried to cover it, did so most of the time, but the pain was still there, hidden deep in those smoke-colored eyes, and even deeper, she suspected, in his heart.

For the first time in more years than she cared to remember, Kendall felt a stirring in her own heart for someone else's pain.

With a finger to her lips, Esther opened the next door. "This is Becca's room."

Kendall peeked in, noting the cheery nursery-rhyme decor and the crib with the sleeping child. Curly hair the same dark color of her father's framed a cherub face that in the darkened room was as angelic as anything Kendall had ever seen. The side rail was down, and she couldn't help remembering that the sheriff had told her the child would soon be three years old. Why was she still in a crib? She didn't have a chance to ask before Esther closed the door and moved on down the hall.

"Jake's room." Esther turned and pointed to the three doors on the opposite side of the hall. "Josh's, Timmy's, and Matt's." She opened each door as she ticked off the names, giving Kendall a brief glimpse of each room before they headed back down the stairs.

"Becca will sleep till mid-afternoon, so that gives me time to acquaint you with the kitchen. Oh, yes," she said as though she'd just remembered something. "Jake has a cleaning service come in to do all the heavy cleaning. You know, vacuuming, mopping, waxing, stripping the floors, cleaning the windows, changing the linens, that sort of thing. And Mavis Reardon picks up the ironing every Tuesday morning before noon and has it back late Wednesday afternoon."

"Do the children have specific chores, or do they take turns—"

"Heavens, no," Esther interrupted, seemingly aghast. "Becca's too young and the boys are much too busy with school and athletics."

"You mean they don't have any responsibilities around the house?"

"Certainly not since I've been here. Besides, with the cleaning crew and ironing done outside, I have to earn my salary somehow." Esther quickly began to clear away the dishes, but Kendall couldn't dismiss it that easily. She could see that she had her work cut out for her, but it was too soon to start making changes. So she made a mental note and stepped in to help. In a matter of minutes they were sitting at the table going over recipes and talking about the Sentell children.

Brad, she already knew, was the oldest and was away at college, though he managed to come home for holidays and an occasional weekend. Josh, the fifteen-year-old, loved football and track, and thirteen-year-old Timmy was their star basketball player. Matt had turned ten last month and was heavy into photography, and both he and Timmy had martial arts classes two nights a week.

Kendall filed away each scrap of information with a growing sense of what-have-I-gotten-myself-into? Four children at home, two of them teenagers, to get to know and to earn their respect and cooperation. There was so much she needed to know and so little time. She was grateful that Esther had taken a liking to her and would freely tell her everything she needed to know. So caught up were they in their growing camaraderie that both were startled by the tiny voice that spoke from behind them.

"My hungry, Esser."

Esther was on her feet immediately. "Baby, you know you're not supposed to climb out of your bed alone. You should have called me." She scooped up the child, who rubbed both eyes, then wrapped her arms around Esther's neck and snuggled close.

"I want you to meet someone," Esther said, carrying Becca back to the table where Kendall still sat. "Becca, this is Kendall. She's going to be staying here to help you take care of your brothers after I leave."

Becca gave Kendall a wary look, then buried her face in the crook of Esther's neck again.

Something told Kendall this wasn't going to be easy. From all she'd put together, Esther O'Malley was the closest thing to a mother Becca had ever known.

"Hi, Becca," she ventured, taking care to speak softly. "Esther tells me you like horses and swimming."

Becca's head came up, her sleepy green eyes lighting up with interest. She nodded her head, sending her long, dark curls bouncing. "My have to wait for Josh to take me," she said through a wide yawn.

Kendall stood and reached for Becca. "I love to ride, and swimming is great exercise. If it's okay with you and Josh, I can take you every day." Becca beamed and leaned into Kendall's waiting arms.

"We have a heated pool out back," Esther told Kendall with a smile of approval. "If you want Becca to show you around, I'll fix a snack and bring it out in a few minutes. Josh has a track meet today, but Timmy and Matt should be getting home soon. They're always starving. Becca, I'll bet Kendall would love to see the horses, too."

Kendall gave Esther a look of thanks. She was giving her and Becca a chance to get to know each other. "Sounds great."

Becca's hand in Kendall's felt small and warm—and

Kendall was touched by the way the child seemed to accept her without question. This might not be so bad after all. Esther had already told her that as much as she adored all the Sentell children, she'd always felt guilty that her age and a bad knee kept her from doing more with them. That Kendall was young and healthy was an added asset.

The pool just beyond the back porch was large and beckoning, but Becca had other ideas.

"C'mon, Kenna," Becca entreated, tugging at Kendall's hand. "Go see horses."

The way the child said her name made Kendall smile. "Kendall's kind of hard for you to say, isn't it, Becca?"

"Uh-huh."

"That's okay. My little sister couldn't say it either. Why don't you just call me Kenny, like she did?" She returned the smile that lit up Becca's face.

"Okay, Kenny."

No sooner had they reached the barn and made a quick round of the stalls than Kendall heard a bell pealing from the house.

Becca grabbed her hand and began pulling her toward the door. "That means come'n get it."

"Well, we'd better go and get it." Kendall bent down and picked up Becca. "Tell me about your brothers," she said, heading toward the patio, where she saw Esther placing a tray on the table shaded by a large yellow and white umbrella. "Brad's the oldest, right?"

"Uh-huh. Josh got his room after he go to kaw . . . kaw . . ."

"College," Kendall helped her out, noting the child's difficulty with the letter L. She'd noticed twin beds in one of the bedrooms earlier and could imagine the hoopla when the next-to-oldest boy inherited his very own room.

"I'll bet Timmy was glad to get the room to himself when Josh moved into Brad's room," she ventured, actually guessing at the living arrangements.

"Uh-huh. Ever'body gots their own room now. Brad sweeps in the big room when he comes home."

The big room. Jake and Becky's bedroom. The room Kendall would be staying in until she could move downstairs and into Esther's quarters. Why was it bothering her to think about sleeping in the same room, probably the same bed, Jake had shared with his wife?

She shook the thought away. "And Matthew? Tell me about Matthew."

Becca gave her a big, toothy grin. "Matt's my bestest friend. He wikes to go swimming with me, but we gotta wait for Josh or Timmy, 'cause they're bigger." Obviously she wanted to make that perfectly clear.

"Well, not anymore. As soon as I get the routine down and the weather's warm enough, we'll go swimming every day, okay?" The sparkle in Becca's eyes was all the answer Kendall needed. Until she got her first paycheck and could buy a bathing suit, shorts and a halter top would have to do. There was no way she was going to disappoint this child for lack of appropriate swimming apparel.

From the road, she heard children calling and looked up to see a school bus stopped at the end of the long drive. Becca squirmed free to race toward the two boys bounding off the bus.

"Come see Kenny," she called to her brothers. "She's gonna take me swimmin' ever'day."

Kendall waved, then headed toward Esther. "She's such a doll," she said to Esther, watching the way

Becca and Timmy and Matt talked and roughhoused down the drive.

"Yes, she is. I'll see to it that you two get to spend as much time as possible together this week." The melancholy in Esther's voice made Kendall look her way. Cutting the apron strings was going to be hard on everyone.

"Thank you, Esther. I have a feeling that your leaving isn't going to be easy, especially for Becca."

"I've got a gut feeling it's going to be quite a shock to Jake, too."

There wasn't time to question Esther's cryptic remark before the energetic threesome was upon them.

"All right, you three," Esther gently scolded. "Settle down and say hello to Kendall Jamison." After the introductions, she told them to all sit down while she went back inside for ice for the soft drinks.

Becca climbed into Kendall's lap without an invitation while Timmy and Matt drew up their chairs directly across the table from her. Neither boy deemed it necessary to hide his curiosity. Timmy brushed back a shock of blond hair and met Kendall's eyes with a cool hazel gaze. Matt, shorter than his brother by a good six inches, studied her just as intently. His eyes were the same color as his brother's, but his hair was as dark as his father's.

Finally Matthew spoke up. "I don't think Josh is going to like this."

Kendall's heart sank. Maybe she'd been premature in thinking things would go well.

"I don't think Josh is going to like this at all." Timmy was as serious as his older brother.

Becca turned to look up at Kendall with wide-eyed innocence. "What's Josh not gonna like, Kenny?"

"I'm not sure, Becca." Kendall matched the boys stare for stare, then gave them her most engaging smile. "But I *am* sure that it's not anything we can't work out. Together."

THREE

Being on call twenty-four hours a day, seven days a week, had been Jake's salvation since Becky's death. He'd always prided himself on being a working sheriff, not just an administrator, a figurehead. Long hours in the field or in his office catching up on tedious paperwork occupied his time to the extent that for a while it blocked out everything else. Today, though, for the first time in longer than he cared to admit, he was anxious to get home. Not that he didn't love his children and cherish every moment he spent with them. It was just having to climb those stairs every night and pass *that* door. . . .

He cursed and stood to pace the width of the room. Again. He pulled up short, then made the trip back to his desk to stare down at the photo of his family. It had been almost three years, for Christ's sake. Why couldn't he just put the past where it belonged and go on with his life? In the beginning, his only reason for halfway trying had been the kids, but they had all recovered with the resilience only the young possess, leaving him alone in his state of emotional limbo.

A day didn't pass that he didn't thank his Maker for his brother and his sister-in-law. If it hadn't been for them and the housekeeper Becky had found early on in her pregnancy, he'd have been tempted to cut it all loose. And it would have been so easy. Becky's folks had wanted to take the children in, help out until Jake was back on his feet. Physically. Mentally. Emotionally.

In his head he knew her death had been no one's fault; in his heart, however, he found it difficult to look past his part in what had happened. He should never have been swayed by Becky's insistence that they could be careful. He could understand her not wanting the tubal ligation the doctor advised. It would have been another surgery for her to endure after Matt's cesarean birth, and no matter how dead set against the vasectomy she'd been, he should have gone ahead with it. If he had—

He grimaced at the memory of hitting the bottle so heavily those first few months. Everyone had been concerned, but it had taken Jared's literally knocking some sense into him to make him realize that the life he and Becky had worked so hard to build over their seventeen years together was slowly going down the toilet. If Jake wanted to go down, Jared had yelled at him, that was his business. But he wasn't taking Jared's nephews and niece with him. How his job had survived, Jake still wasn't sure, but he would be eternally grateful to his twin brother for the thrashing that had set him straight.

After that particularly physical altercation, things had gone better than expected. Esther kept his house going, tended to his children, was doing a remarkable job with Becca. Now, just as he thought everything was on an even keel, exit Esther and enter one Kendall Leigh Jamison. What was he going to do about her? What exactly *was* there to do about her?

He was caught between the proverbial rock and hard place. Esther had to leave Saturday. None of the other prospects had been remotely acceptable. Kendall—Jamison, he corrected himself—wasn't exactly what he'd had in mind. He supposed that subconsciously he'd been looking for another Esther O'Malley. But how many grandmother types do you pull out of Texas penal institutions? Not many, he could vouch for that.

On his desk, Kendall's—dammit, *Jamison's*—file still lay open, seeming to mock his every thought. He'd gone over it again and again since coming back to his office and hadn't found a damned thing that would warrant changing his mind about hiring her.

Face it, Sentell, he rebuked himself, *she's more than qualified for the job. What's more, she's just what you need to convince the finance committee that the reentry program needs to be given a second chance.*

He glanced at his watch. Timmy and Matt had been home over an hour now. He wondered how they were getting along with Jamison. Becca would be a pushover for anyone who showed her half an ounce of attention, but the boys, especially Josh, would be another matter.

Speaking of Josh, if he left now, he could swing by the field house, pick up his son, and break the news before he came face to face with Jamison.

Suddenly Jake wasn't looking forward to going home anymore.

Kendall stood in the doorway of the family room, watching the three children argue over the remote control to the television.

"Give it to me, Becca." Timmy yanked the control from his sister's hands. "You get to watch anything you want to all day long. We're watching *A Current*

Affair.'' He rolled over to look at Matt. "Tonight they're showing sex crimes of the decade.''

In the beginning, Kendall had decided to sit back and watch, see how the household routine went. All afternoon she'd stood by silently and watched Esther wait on these three children like a doting grandmother. Having been abandoned by her own father, Kendall understood how the older woman might have felt about the motherless children in the beginning. Still, in Kendall's mind, Esther had gone overboard in compensating for Becky's death.

Now she'd seen and heard enough.

"I don't think so,'' she said, stepping around and over three snack trays still lying on the floor in front of the TV. The sooner she exercised some sort of authority, she figured, the sooner she'd establish her place in the household. "Dinner will be ready in a little while. I want you to take your trays to the kitchen, then—''

"Daddy!'' Becca squealed, jumping to her feet and racing out the door and into the kitchen. Kendall watched the sheriff swing his daughter high overhead, then return the hug that knocked his hat askew.

Timmy and Matt followed suit, leaving Kendall alone with the mess in the den. She listened to the chatter coming from the kitchen, heard Esther exclaim how happy she was that Jake was home for dinner for a change.

"Where's Jamison?'' she heard the sheriff ask.

"Oh, she's in the den, clearing up the snack trays,'' Timmy chimed in. Kendall glanced toward the kitchen to see the boy looking her way, grinning. *The first open challenge.*

She braced herself, then crossed the hall and entered the kitchen, empty-handed. "No, she isn't.'' Timmy dropped his gaze, then raised it again. "She's helping Esther get dinner ready while you three . . ." She stressed her meaning with a pointed glower at each child. ". . . bring your trays back in here." From her side vision, she saw Esther's impending protest. "Isn't that right, Esther?"

Esther threw a concerned glance at Jake, who looked at Kendall, then nodded to the older woman.

"Kendall's right, children. Straighten up your mess, then wash up for supper." That Esther didn't approve was evident, but she did nothing to undermine Kendall's authority.

"This must be Josh." Kendall broke the uneasy silence by approaching the boy lagging behind Jake. "I'm Kendall," she introduced herself with a smile and an extended hand. "I hear you're our track star."

Josh looked as if he didn't know what had hit him. "Uh, yes, ma'am." He eased his hands into his front pockets, then shifted nervously from one foot to the other. "So, do we call you Kendall or what?"

Kendall laughed. "I think I like Kendall a whole lot better than What." The ice was broken as a slow grin crept across Josh's slightly flushed face.

"Josh, would you mind helping the boys with Becca?" Esther asked. "I think they're both 'bout wore out with her."

"Sure thing," Josh answered with a glance at Kendall as he headed for the stairs.

"That's the damnedest thing I ever saw." The sheriff looked as perplexed as a man could look. "How'd you do it?"

Esther just smiled and returned to the stove.

"Do what?" Kendall hadn't the faintest idea of what he was talking about.

"Josh was the one I was most worried about, and you charmed the socks off him."

Kendall smiled. "Good to know I haven't lost my touch." She sobered at the look that wiped the confusion off the sheriff's face. "What's wrong?"

"Something I hadn't even thought about till now." He'd gone from perplexed to serious so fast that it stunned Kendall. "Esther, how long till supper?"

"Fifteen or twenty minutes."

"Good. Come with me, Jamison." He led the way to the den, where he slid the doors shut behind them. Whatever he had on his mind was serious, if the scowl that covered his face was any indication.

Kendall waited for him to collect his thoughts. When he didn't speak right away, she decided to take the initiative. "What's the matter?"

The sheriff paced the width of the room, then stopped to look at her. "I hate to put a damper on things your first night here, but I think we could be facing a big problem where Josh is concerned."

Kendall wasn't sure she'd heard him right. "But you just said—"

"Never mind what I said and listen to what I'm saying." A sheepish grin replaced his scowl. "Sorry. That didn't make a hell of a lot of sense. I just hadn't counted on Josh's reaction to you—as a woman."

"What do you mean, reaction? You said yourself that he liked me."

The sheriff ran his hand through his hair in a gesture that left no doubt to his exasperation. "Maybe a little too much. He's fifteen years old, Jamison. Hasn't even gone out on his first date yet, but when he saw you just now—"

"You can't be serious." She wanted to laugh, but his solemn expression was no laughing matter. "All right," she said, deciding to give him the benefit of a doubt. "For the sake of argument, let's say he's . . . smitten. I'm twenty-nine years old and think I can handle the situation without causing irreparable damage to his youthful male ego. He may be young, but I'd bet my bottom dollar that he's had crushes on older women before. You know, teachers, friends' sisters, movie stars."

"Yeah," he agreed readily enough. "But there's one big difference. Those women aren't living in the same house, sleeping just down the hall."

One of the things she'd liked about this man from the onset was that he was open and aboveboard. She couldn't find it in her heart to be angry with him. After all, he was a concerned father, looking out for his child's welfare.

"Look, Sheriff, I can understand how you must feel, but I'm not a woman of questionable morals out to seduce anyone. I'm just a woman who made a mistake a lot of years ago. All I want is a second chance—"

He held up one hand to stop her. "Say no more, Jamison. I apologize. I guess I'm just uptight about things changing around here." He slumped into the recliner. "Esther's been a godsend. It's hard to imagine someone taking her place."

He suddenly looked so tired and defeated that Kendall wanted to say or do something to ease his mind. But at the same time she knew she had to make her own position clear.

"That's perfectly understandable," she began, choosing her words carefully. "However, I need to be given a chance if the children, especially the boys, are going to accept me. If they sense that you're having doubts, any doubts at all, it's going to make things that much more difficult." Her heart did a double somersault when he graced her with a weary but devastating smile that drew her attention to his white-white teeth and lips that were full and inviting. For a moment she lost her train of thought when her own words came back to taunt her. *I'm not out to seduce anyone.* In a mindless, self-induced stupor, she watched him come to his feet and approach her.

"You're absolutely right," she heard him say over the roar in her ears. "And I'm not being fair. Let's start over and see if I handle things better this time." He held out his right hand. "Welcome to my home, Jamison."

His apology would have been perfect if he'd called her Kendall, she thought dizzily, taking his proffered hand. It was their first physical contact, and the instant his fingers closed around hers, she was stunned by the intensity of feelings that bombarded her. Large and warm to the touch, his grip was firm, yet gentle. Every nerve ending in her body seemed to transplant itself in her hand, where it acted as a conductor for the sensations that pulsed through her. Five years without close proximity to a man was a long time, but this was ridiculous. She felt her body flush with warmth, and for a moment that seemed like eons, her brain ceased to function. And all from something as innocent as a casual handshake.

"Are you all right?"

She jerked her head up to see concern etched into his furrowed brow. His eyes—Lord, what clear gray eyes he had—studied her so intently that she feared for a moment he might be able to read her thoughts as easily as words on a page. Immediately she dropped her gaze but didn't have the presence of mind to retrieve her hand.

Before she could answer, the doors behind them slid

open. An awkward moment preceded Josh's announcement that supper was ready. Kendall was at a loss over the expression on Josh's face until she saw his gaze riveted to his father's hand still coupled with hers. The sheriff noticed at the same time, and together they broke the contact with thinly veiled embarrassment.

"Great," the sheriff calmly said. "I'm starved." He waited for Kendall to leave the room, then followed with Josh at his side.

The huge country kitchen was alive with the sounds of sibling chatter until Kendall preceded the sheriff and Josh into the room. She stood just inside the door, waiting for everyone to take his accustomed place at the table she'd set earlier.

Everyone watched her, seeming to wait for someone else to make the first move. Finally Becca broke the silence with her choppy baby talk.

"Who make the table pretty?"

"Kendall thought it would be nice if we all had supper together tonight," Esther answered, sending warning glances to each of the boys.

"Why?" Timmy sounded incredulous. "We always take our trays to the den and watch TV while we eat." Another outright challenge.

"Well, not tonight, son." The sheriff took control of the impending bad situation.

"But, Dad," Matt tried to put in, but a scowl from his father stopped his protest.

"Now, children," Esther interceded before the sheriff lost his temper. "Kendall's gone to a lot of trouble to make things nice. Aren't the flowers pretty?"

Three boys exchanged glances that were clearly mutinous.

Kendall felt perfectly awful for being the cause of dissension on her very first night. "It's all right—"

Suddenly she realized she didn't know what to call him. Sheriff had seemed appropriate until now, but Mr. Sentell just wouldn't cut it with her. And Jake seemed too personal under the circumstances.

"Jake," he helped her out, seeming to sense her predicament. "And it won't hurt any of us to sit down at the table together for a change.'"

Grumbling to themselves, the boys took their places on one side of the long kitchen table, while Esther helped Becca with her booster seat, then sat next to her.

"My want Kenny next to me."

"Kenny?" Jake asked.

"She has a hard time with Kendall, so I told her to call me Kenny," Kendall volunteered, exchanging seats with Esther.

"Kenny's sister could'n say it either." Becca smiled up at Kendall, who darted a glance at Jake.

If he caught the reference to Courtney, a sister she wasn't supposed to have, he chose not to show it. Instead, he sat calmly at the head of the table, leaving the chair at the far end empty. After asking the blessing, he handed the plate of fried chicken to Kendall, who put a drumstick on Becca's plate, chose a thigh for herself, then passed the plate to Esther. And around it went until coming back to Jake. Mashed potatoes, cream gravy, green beans, and salad followed. Soon everyone's plate was full and the meal began.

"This tea's great, Esther," Jake said, setting his glass down. "Not as sweet as it usually is."

"Kendall made it," Esther replied. "I didn't know you liked less sugar."

Kendall felt her stomach churn. *Oh, no*, she thought, *not another problem.*

"I like Esther's tea." Timmy defended Esther more valiantly than the champions of the Alamo.

"Yeah," Matt agreed.

"Would you two grow up?" Josh growled. "If you like it sweeter, just add some sugar to it."

Kendall gave him a smile of thanks, and that was the end of that.

Near the end of the meal, however, an uncomfortable feeling settled like a shroud around Kendall. Looking up, she found Josh watching her closely. Embarrassed, he dropped his gaze, and she glanced at Jake and saw that he hadn't missed it either. Perhaps Jake had been right about Josh, she thought. This might well be a problem she didn't need.

After supper, Jake sought the sanctuary of his study. Down the hall he could still hear the boys arguing over what to watch on TV. Suddenly it became quiet, not an easy task to accomplish, he knew. He heard Jamison taking charge. Homework first, she told them, brooking no argument, then one hour of TV before bed.

He had to give her credit. She was good. During their meal, she'd gently steered the conversation from child to child, getting to know each of them individually. And she hadn't been placating them. She'd seemed genuinely interested.

By the time dessert was served, Timmy and Matt had forgotten that she was replacing their beloved Esther and responded to her with a growing sense of acceptance.

Josh, on the other hand, had been uncharacteristically quiet, had only spoken when spoken to. And when Jamison tried to pull him into the conversation, he'd become sullen and excused himself. Homework had never been at the top of his priorities before, and Jake wondered at his second-oldest son's excuse for leaving the table so abruptly.

A light knock sounded at his door, interrupting his thoughts. "Yes," he called in answer.

The doors glided open and Jamison entered with a freshly scrubbed and pajama-clad Becca in her arms. "Becca's ready for bed and wants her daddy to tell her a story."

She put the toddler down, and Jake smiled at the familiar sound of Becca's tiny feet padding across the hardwood floor. Seconds later she sat cuddled in his lap, her busy hands seeking any hidden treasure they might find in his shirt pockets. From the corner of his eye, he saw Jamison quietly leaving them alone.

Becca saw her, too. "Can Kenny stay?"

It was quite possibly the fastest win-over in Sentell history, Jake thought as he turned his head to invite Jamison in for story-telling time. "If she wants to." He indicated one of the wing back chairs on the other side of his desk. He didn't miss the pleased expression on her face, or that she looked tired. Tired and inexplicably happy and fulfilled.

"What do you want to hear tonight, Snuggle Bug?" he asked his daughter, who had slid to a reclining position across his lap. Her head rested in the crook of his arm as she smiled up at him with careless charm.

"Wanna hear Stowry-That-Neber-Ends."

Jake's head fell forward in mock exhaustion. "Becca, that's the longest story on the face of the earth. How about—"

"Stowry-That-Neber-Ends," Becca insisted.

Jake looked up to see Jamison quickly wipe the smile off her lovely face.

"Okay. The Story-That-Never-Ends it is." He stretched his long legs, leaned back in his chair and began.

Fifteen minutes later he silently cursed himself for ever having made up the tale in the first place. Its only saving grace was that if he spoke in low, even tones Becca always fell asleep long before the "and they lived happily ever after" not one of his children had ever heard.

In the quiet of the richly paneled room, his voice at last lulled the tired toddler to sleep. Glancing up, he saw Jamison's gaze on him, saw also the softening of her features as she too listened to the story that had entertained each of his children over the years. When she realized he'd stopped talking and had seen her watching him, her face flushed a most becoming shade of pink. She stood and would have been out the door if Becca hadn't stirred and spoken through a sleepy yawn.

"My want Kenny to tuck me in."

Without having to be asked, Jamison turned back to take the dozing child in her arms. Her hands brushed Jake's chest; his arms grazed her breasts in the exchange, and they both seemed rooted where they stood.

"I have her," Jamison finally said, shifting Becca into a more comfortable position.

Jake couldn't for the life of him understand what happened to him each time they touched. Earlier, in the den, when he'd taken her hand, it had been the same way. Trite though it sounded, time had stood still, giving him free rein to take in every detail of her makeup-free features: skin as clear and fresh as a teenager's, eyes bright and so blue that the clear Texas sky paled in comparison, and full, soft lips that parted in surprise, waiting, it seemed, for his to take possession of them.

He could have stood there forever simply looking at her, but a movement drew his attention to the door, where he got a glimpse of Josh's back disappearing around the corner. How long had the boy been there watching them? What must he have thought?

Jamison obviously hadn't seen Josh and made her way out of the study and up the staircase to Becca's room. *Don't be a jackass*, Jake warned himself, knowing intuitively that he shouldn't follow. Self-advice unheeded, he took the stairs two at a time, hardly noticing the first door on the left this time. He found Jamison lowering Becca into her crib.

The woman was like a magnet drawing him to her, and finally he stood at her side, gazing down at the sleeping bundle of energy and mischief that was his daughter.

"I've never seen anything so beautiful," Jamison whispered in the night-light lit room. Her voice drew his gaze to her face, so soft and lovely in the darkness.

"Yeah," he said, unable to believe the thoughts going through his mind. He looked down to see her hands resting on the side rail and had to consciously keep his hand from closing over hers.

Suddenly she looked at him, and he knew she saw the war waging inside him.

"You've done a remarkable job raising your children," she said, her voice just above a whisper.

He was thankful that she chose to ignore what they both knew was happening between them. "The credit goes to Esther," was all he seemed able to say.

"Yes, Esther's done a fine job, with a few exceptions," she said, breaking off with a guilty downward cast of her eyes.

"What do you mean?"

"I'm sorry. I shouldn't have said that. I've only been in the house a few hours."

"Evidently long enough to have an opinion about how things are run around here."

"Well, yes," she said, glancing down at the sleeping child. "But I think I'll keep my thoughts to myself a while longer. After all, I have to give you all a chance, don't I?"

He felt his lips turn up in a smile that felt great. Other than his children, few things truly made him smile anymore.

"I kept waiting for you to bring up my past during supper," she said, giving him a chance to get his thoughts under control.

"I decided to wait until Esther's gone. That'll give them all time to get to know you." He couldn't keep his eyes from wandering over her fair features again. "In the long run," he said, "I think it'll make it easier for everyone."

He could tell by the doubtful look on her face that she wasn't sure she agreed, but she let it go.

"By the way," she said after a short silence. "That's a wonderful story. I've never heard it before."

"No one except the Sentell children ever have. It started when Brad was younger than Becca is now and has grown with each of them." He chuckled. "I don't know why I always balk at telling it. None of them has ever lasted long enough to hear the ending."

"Is there an ending?" she wanted to know.

"There's always an ending, if someone wants to stick around long enough to hear it." Standing there in the darkened room beside a woman he'd known less than twelve hours, Jake felt something he had never expected to feel again . . . that he was no longer alone.

FOUR

Kendall hated lies and deceit and knew that she was guilty of both. Which had to account for sleep eluding her for the second night in a row. She could understand last night; her nerves had been frazzled from worrying about this morning's interview. Tonight, after tucking Becca in and leaving Jake in the hallway, she'd gone straight to her room to unpack her meager belongings, shower, and fall exhausted into bed. Only she hadn't been able to sleep any more than she had the night before. In fact, she'd tossed and turned until she wanted to pound the bed in frustration.

In her own defense, she argued with herself, she hadn't out and out lied to the sheriff. Still, she couldn't deny that she *had* deliberately misled him. *Deceit*. To make matters worse, she wasn't even sure why. Her records listed no next of kin, which wasn't exactly the truth. *The lie*. Biologically, Courtney wasn't related to her, but seven years of living together under the same roof had forged a bond almost as strong as blood. At least as far as Kendall was concerned.

And, of course, she couldn't discount this *thing*, this *pull*, between Jake and herself. Even now the memory of his touch, first on her hand, then later, when his arm had brushed her breasts as she took Becca from him, sent a wave of warmth oozing through her.

Stop it! She attempted to quell the thoughts by flouncing onto her other side and trying to get more comfortable.

Everyone was settled in for the night, and considering the amount of noise four active children generated when awake, the silence in the big old house verged on being eerie. A wistful smile crept across her face. Ever since she could remember, she'd wanted sisters or brothers, siblings to share laughter and secrets, good times and bad. The loneliness of living in a dysfunctional household—even now, she couldn't use the word *home* to describe her early family life—had left Kendall with a deep-seated yearning that would have crippled anyone with less emotional fortitude.

With a frustrated sigh, she rolled to her other side in the king-size bed, then punched up her pillow before settling back in. Why was she doing this to herself? Dredging up her unhappy past wasn't her style any more than was feeling sorry for herself. So her father had deserted her, and Ellis had used, then discarded her. These things happened. Her years at Gatesville had given her time to put it all into perspective.

She remembered her father as a fun-loving, affectionate man, but he'd never been one to face the hardships of life. When the going got tough, he'd cut and run.

And Ellis . . . well, taking Courtney with him, no doubt, had been part of his scheme to ensure Kendall's cooperation. If the law tracked him down, they'd also find Courtney. And Courtney wasn't the innocent Kendall had been. From the time Courtney was in grade school she'd been in trouble with school officials, graduating to brushes with the law by age eleven. For something as serious as fraud, Courtney undoubtedly would have been looking at a stiff prison sentence, something Kendall couldn't let happen, considering the baby Courtney had been carrying. Ellis's baby.

How had she been so blind? She should have known, sensed that Ellis wasn't all he seemed, especially when he insisted on keeping their relationship a secret. Oh, how she'd loved him—or thought she'd loved him. Had it not been so, she never would have confided in him her deathbed promise to her mother that she would always look after Courtney. And Ellis had used her loyalty to Courtney to ensure her silence. His ploy had worked, and she had paid the price, was still paying the price.

Stop it, she ordered herself and flung back the sheet. Things weren't exactly wonderful, but she was getting on with her life. Again she said a silent thank you that Nancy had learned of Rosemont's reentry program. Where parole officers were concerned, Kendall had lucked out. Nancy Bigelow was one of a kind. Still, Kendall found it hard to believe that she'd confided in Nancy about Courtney and that Nancy had listened without passing judgment or giving unasked for advice. They had become friends in the three short weeks they'd known each other, and Kendall missed her terribly.

Across the room, she heard the doorknob turn, then the door opened.

"Kenny?"

Kendall sat up to see Becca standing in her doorway. The hall night-light enabled her to see the toddler rubbing her eyes with the backs of her tiny fists. Kendall switched on the bedside lamp. "What's wrong, sweetie?"

"My heard sumpin' under my bed."

Kendall wasn't surprised that Becca wasn't able to sleep. Her appearance today had probably triggered the little girl's realization that her life was about to change.

She smiled and patted the mattress. "I have plenty of room in this big old bed. Would you like to sleep with me tonight?"

Becca didn't wait to be coaxed. She scampered across the room and bounded into bed, settling in alongside Kendall. Gently brushing curly locks of dark hair from Becca's face, Kendall felt a warming in her soul that had been missing since she herself was a little girl. Becca snuggled closer, and in a matter of minutes Kendall felt herself drifting off into peaceful slumber. Her contentment was so complete that she forgot to repress the images of clear gray eyes and full, sensual lips that persisted in filling her sleepy thoughts.

Jake lay awake in his bed. Usually his job occupied his thoughts toward the end of the day, but tonight work was the last thing on his mind. And what—or rather who—was on his mind was making him crazy. He grumbled an expletive and flopped from one side to the other. Still the images wouldn't be banished.

Kendall, sitting across from him this morning, her face schooled into an expression of composure.

Kendall, trying to understand his concern about Josh.

Kendall, laughing with his children at the table earlier tonight.

Kendall, sleeping in the room down the hall.

With another oath that shocked even him, he rolled out of bed to stand at the window. Consciously he tried to bring Becky's image into focus. To his bewilderment, all he saw was puzzled blue eyes and a face he'd come to enjoy looking at far too much in the short time he'd known her. Suddenly he was overwhelmed by emotions both forgotten and new, feelings that threw him completely off balance. He'd known his share of women—girls, actually—before marrying Becky, and he had been faithful to her all the years they were together. After her death, he simply hadn't been interested in anyone else. Until now.

Again he swore, first cursing himself for a fool, then Becky, for leaving him alone and vulnerable. That's when he knew what was eating at him. Alone he could handle. Vulnerable was something he wasn't prepared to face. And in less than twenty-four hours Kendall Jamison had made him feel things he hadn't felt, hadn't wanted to feel, in a long, long while.

This time he cursed Kendall, pulled on his jeans, then headed for his study for a nightcap he really didn't want but desperately needed. He pulled up short in front of Becca's room. The door was open, her bed empty. Quickly checking each of the three rooms on the opposite side of the hall and not finding Becca asleep with one of her brothers, he glanced toward Kendall's room. His gut did a queasy somersault at the sight of the open door.

His bare feet made no sound as he strode toward the guest room—his old bedroom. Sleeping peacefully was his daughter with her head resting on Kendall's breast.

Jamison, dammit! Jamison, Jamison, Jamison, he reminded himself for the hundredth time. In spite of his self-recriminations, he stood there watching for several long moments before he closed the door and went on down for the drink he now needed more than ever.

The next four days passed in a whirl of activity with Esther going over every detail of the Sentell household routine. With a little streamlining, Kendall was sure she would be able to handle things once she was on her own.

She didn't realize just how hectic things had been until Saturday morning when they'd all piled into the family station wagon to see Esther off to the airport, leaving Kendall behind to oversee the movers Jake had hired to take Esther's furniture and belongings to Alabama. Kendall's own furniture wouldn't arrive until the middle of the following week, which was fine with her, since she wouldn't have the money to buy her own linens and odds and ends until she drew her first paycheck.

Her first paycheck. She could hardly wait. No matter that she was used to living on very little, she was weary of the two pairs of jeans, two blouses, one bra, and three pair of panties—cotton panties at that—that had seen her this far.

The sound of a car pulling into the parking spaces behind the house distracted her from her grocery shopping list. She glanced out the screen door to see a sleek white Town Car stop near the pool and did a double take. Was she seeing things? The man who uncoiled himself from the driver's side to open the back door was the spitting image of Jake—right down to the lone dimple she saw come to life in his right cheek when he smiled at the antics of the two toddlers who tumbled out of the car.

"Whoa!" he said with a good-natured laugh and scooped both boys up in his arms. "Simmer down so we can get the life vests on you." He gave each a growling hug and put them back on their feet. "Can you manage?" he asked the lovely brunette corralling a third boy who looked to be the same age as the other two. "I want to let the new housekeeper know we're here."

Finally rounding up the three youngsters Kendall now realized were triplets, the brunette smiled over the top of the car. "I can manage, but don't forget swimming was your idea. *You're* going in with them."

By this time the woman had rounded the front of the car, and Kendall saw that she was very pregnant. And due any day now, if Kendall was any judge. She watched the man give his wife a lingering kiss, then head for the back porch.

Kendall met him at the door. "Mr. Sentell." She smiled when he looked startled. "Forgive me. I heard you drive up. I'm Kendall Jamison." She opened the door, then backed away to allow him entry.

"*You're* Jake's new housekeeper?" Clearly he was more surprised at finding that she wasn't a gray-haired old lady sporting the requisite sensible shoes and support hose than by her unexpected appearance at the door.

"And you're Jake's brother. Twin, I see." She glanced past him to the family surrounding the heated pool in the backyard. "That's quite a family you have there," she observed with a smile he didn't bother to return. Obviously the man had something on his mind. "So, what can I do for you today?"

"Jake said he'd recruited someone from his reentry program to take Esther's place, but he didn't tell me . . ." His words trailed off as his eyes quickly took in every detail of Kendall's jeans-clad frame. He shook his head. "We'd better talk."

Inside, he pulled out a chair for her, and Kendall fought back the odd sensation of watching a man who looked exactly like her boss pace back and forth before her.

He finally stopped and impaled her with a frosty glare that held her immobile. "Look," he began, "I don't know what you did to wind up behind bars, but Jake's had a hard time of it the past three years, and I won't sit by and watch everything he's worked for go down the tube—''

Kendall came to her feet, effectively cutting him off. Being issued a warning from the sheriff in the beginning was one thing, but being bullied by his brother was something else altogether. "Mr. Sentell, all I want is to do my job, earn a living, and get on with my life—''

''Just be careful that you don't do anything that'll cause my brother . . . trouble.''

Standing there, glaring at each other, neither of them heard the door open.

''Jared?''

Kendall pulled her eyes from the carbon copy of her boss to look toward the woman standing just inside the room.

''The boys are waiting for you.'' She spoke softly, but even Kendall heard the unspoken reprimand in her voice. Without another word, or even a glance in Kendall's direction, Jared Sentell stalked back outside.

''I apologize for my husband.'' The woman placed one hand on the small of her back and stretched the muscles there. ''And for taking you by surprise. I talked with Jake this morning, and when he found out the boys wanted to go swimming, he insisted we bring them over. It's still too cool for the creek. We thought it would help take some of the sting out of Esther's leaving if we had a family get-together this afternoon. I guess he forgot to tell you.''

While the other woman explained, Kendall offered her a seat and poured them each a tall glass of iced tea. ''That's okay. It *is* the sheriff's house, after all.

My name's Kendall," she said, placing a glass on the table before her guest.

"Leza," she said, introducing herself and taking a long sip. "That sure hits the spot." She raised her gaze to meet Kendall's once more. "Jared really is a nice guy, and he means well. It's just that they've been through a lot together and they're very protective of each other. And Jared's right. The past three years have been especially hard for Jake. Jared just doesn't want to see his brother hurt."

Kendall admired Jared and Leza Sentell for their loyalty to Jake, but she wasn't about to let them peg her as some sort of heartbreaker. "Like I told your husband, Leza, all I want is to be left alone to do my job." She didn't mean to sound defensive but wasn't surprised that she did.

Leza studied Kendall a moment. "I think you'll do just fine." With all the grace of a pregnant woman, she struggled to her feet. "We brought our own soft drinks and a picnic lunch. Would you like to join us?" When Kendall hesitated, Leza reached out and took her hand. "It might help break the ice with Jared. We're a big part of Jake's life, and it wouldn't hurt if you two got along."

Kendall felt as though she'd made her first friend. "I'd love to. I have ice cream."

Leza's blue-green eyes widened, adding even more charm to the grin that eased across her pert, heart-shaped features. "Blue Bell Cookies 'n' Cream?" Kendall returned Leza's grin with a conspiratorial one of her own. "Oh, Dr. Lauck isn't going to be happy with my weight gain on Friday."

The rest of the afternoon turned into one that Kendall would remember fondly. Jared and Leza's boys— Adam, Mark, and Lucas—were just starting to settle down when the other Sentell clan returned home. Then the fun started all over again. Kendall was enchanted by the closeness the two families shared. Enchanted and a bit envious. She was also amazed at how well the two broods got along, especially considering the wide range of ages. Josh, who still occasionally cast longing glances at Kendall, had his father's and his uncle's patience with the younger children, especially with the triplets and Becca. Timmy and Matt kept pretty much to themselves in the deep end of the pool, practicing their diving and other aquatic tricks.

At last it was time to say good-bye to their company, and Kendall excused herself to go inside when she realized she'd almost invited them to stay for supper. Everyone had made her feel so welcome and accepted— even Jared warmed to her after an hour or so—that she'd almost forgotten she was hired help, not part of the family. Unaccountably, the realization hurt more than she was willing to admit.

Standing at the sink, rinsing the glasses they'd used poolside, she heard the back door open, then close. She didn't have to look to know that it was Jake. Then he was beside her, adding two glasses to the dishwater.

"You should have used the dishwasher," he said, not bothering to step away.

"I keep forgetting you have one," she answered honestly. "I'll get the hang of it." This was one of the few times they'd been alone since they'd tucked Becca into bed that first night. It was still there, the intensity, the awareness of each other, and she wondered if he felt it, too. No sooner did the thought materialize than he stepped away.

He didn't go far. Just out of touching range. "You made my brother and his family feel welcome. Thanks."

"It's your house, Sheriff. I'm here to make things comfortable for your family and friends. It's my job."

"Technically," he agreed. Standing before her in his swim trunks and open shirt, he looked suddenly very uncomfortable and undeniably sexy. "What I meant to say was that you handled things well. I forgot to tell you they were coming over. I'll try not to be so inconsiderate again."

"Thanks." She tried to look him in the eye, but the way he was looking at her made her drop her gaze. Which was a mistake. She'd found it increasingly difficult to keep her eyes off him from the moment he came out of the house wearing his swim trunks. It was the first time she'd seen him in anything other than his uniform, and the sight of his bare chest and arms—not to mention his nicely rounded backside—stole her breath away. Her very active imagination had no trouble visualizing him doing a layout for an underwear commercial. Silently she reprimanded herself. Jared, too, was a fine physical specimen, but she hadn't ogled him like some starry-eyed debutante. Not only was it uncharacteristic of her, but embarrassing as well when she recalled the times Jake had caught her checking him out.

"I have some things to take care of at the office this afternoon," he said, saving her from herself again. "Do you need me to pick up anything for you?"

"As a matter of fact," she answered, drying her hands and going to the table where she'd abandoned her grocery list earlier, "I was planning to go to town myself. There are a few things we need from the market."

"McElvey delivers, if you'd rather use your time for something else."

"No," Kendall replied. "Esther introduced me to the

McElveys earlier in the week, but I'd like to look the store over. Get a better idea of the items they stock.'' Lowering her lashes, she schooled her thoughts. ''It's been a while since I shopped, Sheriff, and I—''

''Enough said,'' Jake said, and surprised them both by laying his hands on her shoulders and squeezing gently.

There it was again, that electrifying jolt of awareness that surged to life whenever they got too close. Until that very moment, she hadn't realized how carefully they had each avoided any physical contact during the week. Of course, it hadn't been that hard. Mornings were hectic with Jake leaving the house shortly after the boys caught the bus for school. And he rarely made it home before bedtime each evening.

Somewhere in the back of her mind, Kendall knew she should step away, stop this before it went further than either of them wanted. But knowing and doing were two different things. All she seemed capable of was raising her eyes to meet his. Which was her second mistake. She saw in eyes that were more gray than blue that he was fighting the same battle that she was losing.

He finally broke the awkward moment. ''Are you sure you want to tackle taking the kids with you on your first trip out alone?''

Relief washed over Kendall that he'd been able to form an intelligible thought when she couldn't. ''Has to be a first time for everything,'' she said with a nervous laugh. ''May as well get it over. Besides, I'm anxious to try out my temporary driver's license.''

''The extra set of keys is hanging inside the cupboard.'' He glanced at the clock on the microwave. ''It's getting late. Why don't you and the kids meet me at the Silverado Steak House for supper around seven?

They have a great buffet and salad bar. Josh knows how to get there.''

Kendall's first thought was her clothes. Her other pair of jeans were clean but as faded and worn as the ones she was wearing. And, of course, her workout sweats wouldn't do. "How should I dress the kids?"

"School clothes will be fine."

"I'd planned to go like this. Are jeans okay?"

"It's a family restaurant. Very casual." Then his featured sobered. "If you're short on cash right now, I can advance you—"

"No," she cut in. "Thank you, but I can wait." She hoped he had no idea of her treks downstairs to the laundry room every other night after everyone else was in bed.

"I'll help you round up the kids and get them ready."

"I can manage," Kendall answered, wondering why she was in such a hurry for him to get dressed and leave. "You said you had work to do, and I have plenty of time. Besides, Josh is pretty good about helping out. See you at seven."

She watched him leave to go up to change and wondered why she'd found it necessary to lead him to believe that Josh was coming around. Things hadn't gone as well as she'd hoped. All week the boy had done nothing but watch her every move as if taking mental notes on the things she did right or wrong. Whatever his problem, it seemed to be rubbing off on Timmy and Matt. Then Esther's constant hovering hadn't helped matters at all. Now that Esther was gone, she'd be able to start her own regimen, something she both dreaded and looked forward to doing.

Standing at the back door, she watched Josh patiently

help Becca paddle across the shallow end of the pool. Now was as good a time as any.

"Josh," she called, opening the screen door and stepping out onto the wide back porch. "Please bring Becca inside, then help your brothers clear away the rest of the dishes while I get her dressed."

Josh's forehead wrinkled, but he helped Becca out of the pool, then hefted himself out of the water. Timmy and Matt stopped roughhousing long enough to throw questioning glances at their older brother. Josh wrapped a towel around his baby sister, picked her up, and carried her toward the house.

After handing Becca over to Kendall, he stepped back, then looked over his shoulder at the two boys still in the pool. Kendall saw him square his shoulders before he faced her again.

"You're the housekeeper," he said, not loudly, but making sure Timmy and Matt heard him. Then he started to sidestep her.

Kendall stepped into his path. She was surprised by this unexpected change in him. He'd been cool and distant at times but had never been outright disrespectful. Maybe it was his way of dealing with the attraction he felt toward her.

"Yes, Josh. I am the housekeeper, but I hope I can count on you to give me a hand from time to time." She said it with all the calm she could muster, knowing that if Josh backed her down in front of the boys, her job was going to be impossible. Seeming to sense that something was wrong, Becca wound her arms around Kendall's neck.

Josh glanced over his shoulder again. His audience was still there, still as attentive as before. When he turned back, his eyes, the same pewter shade as his father's, challenged her. "Esther managed to take care of things without my help."

"Yes," she agreed. "But Esther had an advantage I don't have, Josh." She shifted Becca to her other hip. "She didn't come into your lives to take someone else's place. Your mother needed help and Esther was there when you all needed her." She saw the slight relaxation of his stance; still he wasn't ready to give in.

"Maybe so, but Esther never made us do *her* work. She said the house was her job, that we had enough to do with school and sports.

Kendall knew that losing her temper now would do more harm than good. What she needed now was a cool head and a convincing argument. "Esther's a fine woman," she said, "but children need to have responsibilities around the house." Inwardly she cringed at her poor choice of words.

Josh bristled. "I'm not a child!"

Timmy and Matthew had migrated from the pool to the bottom of the steps behind Josh. Kendall couldn't help noticing the way Josh puffed up his chest, for his brothers' benefit, she was certain. She was losing ground, and losing it quickly. She had to do something.

"I didn't mean to imply that you were." She'd have to think fast to smooth this over. Thank goodness an idea struck her. "Are you a sporting man, Josh?" she asked, eyeing the muscled breadth of his shoulders, the athletic definition of his upper body.

Josh pulled his gaze from his brothers' to the woman in front of him. "What?" Clearly she'd thrown him a curve.

"If I challenge you to, let's say, an arm wrestling match, would you be willing to wager your cooperation against my never asking for your help again?"

Josh looked incredulous. "You're not serious."

From their expressions, Timmy and Matt didn't know what to think either.

"You're not scared, are you?"

That did it. "Scared? Of you?"

Kendall couldn't help smiling. "You can save us both a lot of time and aggravation by accepting my challenge. I need help and I'm going to have it, one way or another."

Having thrown down the gauntlet, she turned and went inside the house. In the kitchen, she pulled a chair away from the table, then took a seat in the one adjacent to it, leaving the corner for the competition she had made sure he couldn't refuse. Carefully setting Becca down beside her chair, she waited for the three boys to follow.

Josh stood in stunned silence before her while the other two backed him up.

"C'mon, Josh. This won't take long." Timmy seemed to be the only one wanting the match to take place. Matt looked from Josh to Timmy to Kendall, then back again.

"This is crazy," Josh said with a shake of his blond head.

Kendall gave his chair a push with her foot. "Crazy or not, unless you're willing to give in, this seems as good a way as any to settle this." She turned her attention to the others. "If Josh wins, things stay the way they've been." She impaled each of them with a look she hoped conveyed her determination. "If I win, you do as I ask whenever I ask. Agreed?"

The only one who had no reservations spoke up. "There's no way she can beat you, Josh." Timmy put his hand on the back of the chair meant for Josh. "Show her." Still Josh hesitated. "You *aren't* scared, are you?" Timmy obviously knew how to handle his older brother. Josh swung his leg over the chair back, took his seat, then leaned forward to place his right elbow on the table.

Kendall took her cue and did the same. They clasped right hands, and their eyes connected. Over Josh's shoulder, she saw Jake standing in the doorway. It was too late to back out now. She readied herself for the contest.

"Ready . . . set . . . go!" Timmy yelled.

Timmy and Matt shouted words of encouragement for their brother while Becca pulled for both of them. The look on Josh's face said plainly that Kendall's strength surprised him but that he was confident he could take her. He gripped the edge of the table with his free hand, and his face contorted with the effort. She had no doubt that Josh was physically stronger, but his youth and inexperience would work against him. She hoped he thought he could beat her with brute strength alone.

Positioning her left foot and leg to her advantage, she leaned forward, unobtrusively angling her shoulder and upper body into the grip for added leverage, a technique that had served her well in prison. The muscles all over his body tensed, but she knew she could easily take him. After all, she'd been the arm wrestling champion at Gatesville for the last three years.

Slowly, surely, her hand passed the upright position, forcing Josh's forearm backward. Strong though he was, she knew she was only seconds away from victory.

His eyes darted to his brothers, who had grown uncharacteristically quiet, then back to Kendall's straining biceps. He raised his gaze to hers, then, embarrassed, he lowered it.

In that instant Kendall realized her mistake. If she

won out over Josh now, caused him to lose face with his siblings, she would never be able to live with herself. Or with him.

Careful not to make it too obvious, she began to let up. She saw the surprise in his face when he was slowly able to drive her forearm backward. Timmy and Matt began to cheer with renewed fervor, howling in victory the instant Kendall's arm crashed to the table. The two younger boys danced and clapped Josh on the back. Becca, too, celebrated, knowing only that someone had won something. Josh reached up with his left hand to massage his arm, his eyes still fastened on Kendall.

She rubbed her own arm, cursing herself for her lack of patience. She hadn't accomplished a thing. If she hadn't pushed this today, she might have earned their help and respect in the long run, but there was no hope now. She stood, feeling that she had failed the children more than anything. Jake, dressed in a crisp white shirt and snug-fitting jeans, didn't say a word. He simply took his hat from the peg by the door and settled it on his head. He was letting her handle this on her own.

The other two boys finally quieted down. Timmy grinned at her with all the smugness of a thirteen-year-old. Matt shifted uncomfortably from one foot to the other. Josh still rubbed his arm.

Kendall reached for Becca. "Congratulations, Josh. Your father's invited us to dinner in town later. If you'll get cleaned up, I'll straighten up down here, then meet you in the den in thirty minutes."

Josh laid his hand on her arm. With a glance at his brothers, he said, "Me and the boys'll straighten up while you and Becca get ready."

"What?" Timmy exclaimed, more than a little dumbstruck.

"*I said* we'd take care of the dishes. Kendall has to

give Becca her bath and dress her." He gave Kendall a smile of thanks that no one saw except her. "It'll save time if we help." He didn't have to say more. The younger boys grumbled between themselves but didn't argue as they followed Josh back outside.

"Nice move."

She'd almost forgotten Jake was in the room. "I don't know what you mean," she said, putting Becca down again.

Jake had the most contagious grin she'd ever seen. "He's a strong boy, but you had him from the beginning. It almost backfired on you, though. If you'd won, none of them would have forgiven you."

"That's not why I—"

"I know." His expression sobered. "Timmy and Matt think Josh is the greatest thing since ESPN. Thanks for not destroying that." He stood in the door and let his gaze slide from her eyes to her bare feet. "I'll keep in mind that you know how to handle yourself," he said, his voice dropping a seductive note. "You might want to remember that I'm not an inexperienced schoolboy, though."

FIVE

Keeping in mind that they wouldn't be going straight home afterward, Kendall kept her purchases to nonperishables. All went well with the children, with the exception of the "great grape fight" between Timmy and Matt in the produce section of McElvey's Grocery Store.

All week long Kendall had kept mental track of some of the things she wanted to change in the Sentell household. Diet was at the top of the list. Esther was a wonderful housekeeper and cook, but her idea of a well-balanced meal included anything fried and vegetables seasoned to taste-bud perfection with salt pork or bacon drippings. And Kendall had been appalled at the amount of sweets the older woman allowed the children to consume in a day's time.

Deciding to take it slow and easy, she'd quietly filled her shopping cart with a select variety of fruits and juices. She had yet to figure out just how to ease cola and junk food out of their diets, but she was determined to give it her best shot.

She spotted the sheriff's patrol car parked in front of the steak house as she maneuvered the station wagon into the parking lot. She glanced at her watch. They were a few minutes early, so she breathed easier knowing she hadn't kept him waiting.

She didn't have to ask Josh to take Becca out of her car seat. He had the toddler in his arms by the time Kendall closed the driver's door. From the moment they'd left the house, Josh had made it his personal business to make things easy for Kendall, which included keeping Timmy in line. The arm wrestling match had turned the tide in her favor. And heaven knew she needed all the help she could get.

Jake stood just inside the door, chatting with the waitress at the register. He smiled when he saw his family, and Kendall had to make a conscious effort to make her heart stop its frantic tattoo beneath her breast.

The petite woman smiling up at him sized Kendall up in one brief once-over. Kendall knew she'd just been tagged as the competition, which made her uncomfortable, especially when the lovely brunette looked as delicate as the roses Rosemont was famous for growing. In comparison, Kendall felt awkward and Amazonian. She'd bet the brunette wouldn't know the first thing about arm wrestling or body building. And, at the precise moment, Kendall wished she didn't. Or maybe it was just that she wished Jake hadn't witnessed her less than feminine side.

"Good, you're here," Jake said in greeting, giving the brunette a parting smile as he approached Kendall and his brood of four. "I'm hungry enough to eat—"

"A buffalo wearing combat boots," all four children chimed in. Obviously it was an inside joke, but the way they all smiled at her didn't make her feel like an outsider at all.

Jake laughed, and the sound was quite possibly the most endearing thing Kendall had ever heard. She fell in behind the boys while Jake took charge of his daughter.

The restaurant, typical of Texas steak houses, was large and crowded with booths and tables. Jake led the way to the nonsmoking section. Once settled in at the largest table in the center of the room, they gave their drink orders to the waitress, fortunately not the brunette talking to Jake earlier. Then they began the trek around the buffet and salad bar.

Jake hadn't misled her. Kendall had never seen so many entrées and vegetable dishes in one place in her life. Fried chicken, barbecued beef, fried and baked fish, boiled shrimp, green and baked beans, mashed potatoes and potato salad, corn on the cob, eggplant casserole, and much, much more tempted Kendall as she made her way around the steam table. Then there was the dessert section. Pecan, coconut, chocolate, and apple pies; blackberry and peach cobblers and soft ice cream. The salad bar was equally well stocked, and soon everyone had prepared his own plate and met back at the table.

Dinner was an unhurried affair with plenty of lively conversation, most of which centered on the boys and their school work and athletics. Josh was so like his father that Kendall found herself thinking how lucky any girl would be to be the object of his attention. And Jake—well, Jake was about as perfect as men came, at least in Kendall's meager experience.

Across the room an elderly couple sitting in a booth caught her eye. Ever since she was a small girl, she'd been a people watcher, and old habits had a way of sticking around. From the moment she noticed them quietly talking, Kendall began fantasizing about their lives together. They'd been childhood sweethearts who married in their teens, she decided, had three married children, two sons and one daughter, who all lived right here in Rosemont, eight grandchildren, and they would soon celebrate their golden anniversary. As she'd noticed him do before, the balding old man smiled at his wife and reached across the table to pat her weathered hand affectionately. The woman laid her hand over his and gave it a gentle squeeze.

Another adoring smile and the elderly gentlemen scooted across the vinyl seat, stood, and extended his hand. His wife shook her silver-gray head and stubbornly tried to stand alone. Her legs wobbled a bit, then gave way. Undaunted, she gave it another try. Same result. Again she smiled up, this time sheepishly, then took the hand that was still there—had always, would always be there—and came to her feet.

Kendall felt the sting of tears in her eyes. Until that very moment, she hadn't realized that what they had was all she'd ever wanted in life. Someone to love and love her in return, someone to share days and nights and dreams and disappointments. *Forever*. She'd dared to hope she'd found all that with Ellis. How wrong she'd been.

Glancing away from the couple, she was unnerved to find Jake's gaze on her. He too had watched the little drama across the way, and she hoped the longing she felt didn't show in her face.

She lowered her head and didn't see the couple approach their table until the old man spoke. "You have a fine family, young man," he said to Jake, his faded hazel eyes taking in each child in turn before coming to rest on Kendall. "Enjoy every minute with them."

Jake's gaze swept the table but came to rest on Kendall's flushed face. "Thank you, sir. I will," he answered without bothering to explain that Kendall wasn't his wife.

"Well," Jake said to break the awkward moment after the couple left, "can I interest anyone in dessert?"

"Me, me, me," Becca squealed, bouncing in her seat.

Jake laughed and took Becca by the hand. Kendall watched the trail of Sentells heading for the dessert bar. She wouldn't hazard a guess to how her father would have reacted, but she knew her stepfather would have punished Courtney or herself for behaving so spontaneously by forbidding them their dessert. Ellis would have been mortified by the child's outburst of delight. The more Kendall saw and learned of Jake Sentell, the more there was to like.

"What'cha gonna get, Kenny?" Becca asked, coming back to the table empty handed.

"I think I'll have some watermelon and cantaloupe," she answered, herding Becca toward the fruit at the end of the salad bar. "Do you like fresh strawberries?" she asked the chid.

"I do, I reawwy do," Becca answered, dancing with glee.

By the time she and Becca returned to the table, the boys were going back for seconds. Jake was still enjoying his cobbler à la mode and looked with approval at the plate of fruit Kendall had prepared for his daughter.

"Trying to make a convert?" he asked, watching Becca devour a strawberry so large that Kendall had to quarter it in order for the child to get it in her mouth.

"Do you mind?"

Jake shook his head. "Not at all. If the boys weren't so active, I'd have said something to Esther long ago."

While Becca and Kendall finished up, Jake paid the

check, then returned. "Is everyone ready?" he asked, wiping Becca's hands and face. He stood beside Kendall, and when she reached for her purse, she turned to find his outstretched hand waiting to help her to her feet. There was nothing for her to do without calling undue attention to a simple gesture of courtesy, so she slipped her hand into his. She felt everything worth feeling in that brief moment, including the calluses in his palm, the tenderness of a caress yet to come, the tingle of anticipation . . . and that he too ached with the fear of never sharing himself with someone again.

It was past midnight. The kitchen was empty, but Jake heard Kendall milling around in the laundry room. As had happened more often than not of late, he hadn't been able to sleep, so he'd come down for a nightcap, something that could become a bad habit again if he wasn't careful. When he'd seen Kendall's door open and no Kendall, he'd almost changed his mind about taking a chance on running into her. Why tempt fate? But in spite of his good intentions, he'd felt compelled to wait for her.

Drink in hand, he stepped across the threshold and called her name. She appeared in the doorway that connected the utility room to the kitchen, a bundle of folded clothing cradled in her arms. From where he stood, he saw two pairs of jeans, the two shirts she'd alternated wearing all week, and a pair of gray sweats. He also saw several pair of panties and a bra, all sensible white and care-free cotton.

Barefoot, she wore a thin cotton gown that revealed just enough to pique his male interest. Her eyes flickered across his bare chest, then traveled lower to the waistband of his button-up jeans. Embarrassment glowed in her face as she quickly glanced away, but not before he had a chance to glimpse the awakening of desire in her eyes. Suddenly he wished he'd taken the time to slip on his shirt. He was having a hard enough time dealing with his own crazy hormones; he didn't need the added guilt of resurrecting hers.

"I didn't mean to wake you." Her voice washed over him like a caress in the dark.

"You didn't." He tried to sound natural and wasn't surprised that he didn't quite make it. "Guess I ate too much cobbler." Sorry excuse that it was, he wasn't about to admit that erotic thoughts of her had kept him awake every night this week. "Would you like a drink?"

"No, thanks. I made myself some cocoa." She nodded toward the mug on the breakfast bar.

Jake looked down at the drink in his hand. "You know, that sounds pretty good." Stepping to the sink, he poured the bourbon down the drain. He opened one cupboard door, then closed it when he realized he had no idea where the chocolate was kept.

"Here," Kendall offered, placing her stack of laundry on the table. "I'll do it. The water's still hot."

Straddling one of the bar stools, Jake watched her move around his kitchen as if she'd been doing it for years. Her gown was modest enough, almost ankle length with a chaste neckline and long sleeves, but the way it swung with her movements caused it to cling to her nicely rounded curves, curves he wasn't above noticing. He'd wager a year's salary that every pair of panties she owned was sitting on his table at this very moment. His jeans became suddenly less comfortable than they'd been just a few minutes ago.

"There were some messages on the machine when we got home. I wrote them down for you." She indicated the notepad next to the telephone.

He picked up the pad and began flipping the pages. "What's this from Morris Furniture?" he asked, grateful for something else to occupy his wayward thoughts.

"Oh, it's my bedroom furniture. They'll be delivering it Wednesday morning. Then I can move my things downstairs into my own room." She placed his hot chocolate on the placemat in front of him, then picked up her own cup.

"I haven't received a bill for this," he said, taking a sip that almost scorched his tongue.

"And you won't." She sat across from him and wrapped her fingers around her mug. "Esther put in a good word for me, and they agreed to let me pay it out on time."

He should have known she wouldn't let him pay for furniture for her personal use. "One of the nice things about small towns," he said, not at all surprised Gertrude Morris had extended credit to a complete stranger. "I've been thinking," he went on to say, "and have decided to pay you weekly instead of once a month, like we agreed." He wasn't sure how that was going to go over, but if her laundry was any indication, she could use the money now. "I'll leave a check on my desk in the morning." He could tell that she wanted to protest, but common sense won out in the end.

"Thank you. There are a few things I really need." She wouldn't even look at him now, and again he wished he had his shirt.

"I think the children are adjusting well to Esther's leaving today," she ventured after a brief lull in the conversation. "Going out for dinner was a good idea."

A mental image of her face as she watched the old couple at the steak house invaded his mind's eye. For the briefest moment, she'd looked so forlorn that he'd wanted to say or do something to ease whatever had upset her. Then he'd been plagued by his own memories. He'd never considered growing old without Becky. Not once since her death had he entertained the idea of anyone else being with him during his golden years. Now he couldn't imagine anyone there except Kendall. That shocked the hell out of him.

"Yes," he made himself respond calmly. "And so was having Jared's family over this afternoon. I'm glad Leza felt like coming over." Now he was looking for things to say. "Thanks again for putting up with us all."

"They're a lovely couple." She smiled for the first time since he'd come into the room. "And their boys are adorable. I can't help wondering how she's going to manage after the baby comes, though."

"Babies," he corrected. "She's expecting twins."

"You're kidding."

"No, I'm not. But at least they have help. Maggie's been with Jared since he started his ranch over twenty years ago."

Small talk lapsed into another awkward silence. Jake rested his forearms against the edge of the bar while Kendall ran her finger around the rim of her mug.

Finally she spoke. "I hadn't meant to bring this up so soon, but . . ."

When she looked across the bar at him, he realized he was watching her mouth. "But," he prodded, finding it increasingly difficult to ignore her obvious charms.

"Well, Becca's been to my room almost every night this week."

"Sorry she's bothering you. I'll have a talk with her."

"It's not that," she quickly added. "I think the problem is her bed. She's much too old to still be sleeping in a crib.'' She cleared her throat, giving him the impression she intended to say more. He was right. ''I saw several nice beds while I was shopping for mine. I wouldn't mind—''

''No,'' he broke in brusquely, feeling like a heel when she flinched. He'd overreacted, but he liked things the way they were. Becca's room was the last one Becky had decorated before . . .

''Don't try to change everything in one day,'' he said, forcing a smile he hoped would soften his unintentional criticism.

It didn't work. She stood and took her mug to the sink. Jake cursed himself for having spoken so hastily. He hadn't meant to sound harsh, but he didn't like change and she'd taken him off guard.

He followed, stopping behind her, then reaching around her to put his mug in the sink. His bare chest brushed her shoulder and they both froze. From where he stood, he had a perfect view of the gentle slope of her neck.

Her hair, as always, hung in a single French braid down her back. He fought the urge to loosen it and let her hair fall about her shoulders. He could almost feel its rich texture between his fingers. But he couldn't resist the stray tendrils that lay against her nape. Before he had time to consider the consequences, he brushed them aside. His fingers lingered there against her skin, skin that was softer than he'd imagined. Breathing had never been a chore before, he thought, turning her to face him.

Her lower lip quivered ever so slightly and he found himself wanting to draw it between his own lips, gently suck it into his mouth.

''Please, Sheriff,'' she whispered, her eyes downcast. ''This is a complication neither of us needs.''

"Yeah, I know." At the moment, he had no more control over his actions than he did of his hand slowly traveling up the length of her arm.

"This is a mistake." Her voice was husky now, unsteady.

"Maybe." He leaned toward her, stopping a hair's breadth from her lips. "But I'd feel better knowing what we're up against." He hadn't counted on this, but something about her brought the loneliness of the past three years into sharp focus, then made him forget it in the same breath. "Wouldn't you?"

She didn't answer, nor did she resist him.

The instant his lips touched hers, he knew there would be more, much more between them. If not tonight . . .

The first thing he tasted was cocoa. Then there was nothing but the sweet, drugging taste of Kendall. He worked slowly, wanting to memorize everything about this moment: the taste and feel of her pliant lips against his as he slanted his mouth over hers for a deeper, more intimate kiss, the way her tongue retreated at the first contact with his, then came back to tease him, the soft moan that escaped from her mouth to his.

The fresh, clean scent of shampoo and body powder and Kendall lulled him deeper into the magical spell they were creating together. His head argued valiantly with his heart, but it was a losing battle. Until this moment he hadn't really touched her. If he did, he might not be able to stop himself. If he didn't, he would hate himself tomorrow.

Without releasing her lips, he brought his hand to her waist. Her body beneath the flimsy cotton fabric was warm and solid and inviting, and he had to have more.

He closed the distance between them with one step,

letting his hand ease upward from the gentle curve of her hip and waist. His palm curved around her rib cage while his thumb came to rest just below the fullness of her breast. He heard her sudden intake of breath, felt her tremble beneath his touch, and boldly he cupped the soft swell of flesh that grew taut beneath his fingers.

She swayed toward him, her small gasp of surprise at the intimate contact of their bodies inflaming him. She was a little rusty at this, he thought, surprised at how dazed he was. He wasn't foolish enough to think that she'd never had a lover, and he found he liked the idea of being the man to reintroduce her to the art of making love. If she'd responded any differently, come on too strong, he'd probably have bolted like a skittish colt. But she hadn't, and he couldn't help wanting more of her.

Regretfully, now was neither the time nor the place. His children were asleep upstairs, and he had no intention of compromising Kendall's station in his household.

Never had he done anything so difficult, but he broke the contact. Still, he couldn't find the strength to move away from her. He rested his forehead against hers, waiting for strength and sanity to return.

Kendall remained where she stood. "So?" she asked, more than a little breathless. "Are we in trouble, or what?"

Jake felt a chuckle rumbling up from his chest. "Considering this is the first day we've been alone, I'd have to say we're in way over our heads."

When he couldn't seem to move away, Kendall did. She left him to retrieve her laundry from the table. He turned to see her looking at him.

Her skin glowed pink and rosy; her lips were softly swollen. "Now that we know," she began, "I think we'd better try harder to keep our distance. I need this job, Sheriff, and I like your children, but if I have to, I'll start looking for another job tomorrow.'' Her voice was shaky, but her eyes spoke of her sincerity.

He'd known from the outset that he liked her, but he wondered if he would ever get used to her penchant for getting straight to the point. And, dammit, she was right. What he'd let happen—no, what he'd *done*— couldn't happen again. Too much was on the line.

''No, Jamison,'' he said, knowing that the use of her last name following so intimate an encounter would be like a slap in the face. He *needed* her to be angry now. ''Tonight was my fault, and you have my word it won't happen again. Now that we know what we're dealing with, I think we'll be smarter about being in close proximity, especially in the dead of night.''

Her face had paled, but she managed to nod and say a stiff good night. He watched her go, wondering how he was going to keep his word when she was on his mind more and more—and sleeping just down the hall.

Three years was a long time for a man to be without the comfort of a woman's touch, but his attraction to her, he was coming to realize, was much more than a physical thing.

Knowing this, how could he trust himself to keep his hands off her—and, more to the point, his heart to himself?

SIX

True to his word, Jake saw to it that there wasn't a repeat performance of their Sunday morning encounter. Kendall was at once relieved and disappointed when he left each morning before she woke to get the boys off to school, and returned each night in time to tuck Becca in, then spend a little time with the older children. They spoke mostly on the telephone and only about things that pertained to the smooth operation of his household.

Today she'd just gotten Becca down for her nap and was into the cool-down portion of *Vikki Valen's Noonday Aerobic Workout* on Channel 7 when she heard her name called from the back door. Thinking that it was too early for Mavis Reardon to be returning the ironing, she grabbed her towel and walk-jogged to the kitchen.

Leza Sentell smiled at her through the screen door and, with a wide Cheshire-cat grin, held up a bakery box. Kendall grimaced at the thought of how many calories one small box could hold.

She unhooked the latch, and Leza surprised her with a quick, spontaneous hug. The pregnant woman checked out Kendall's trim frame, then gave her a grimace of her own.

"I hate you," Leza teased, patting her very rounded stomach. "I suppose these are a no-no." She opened the box and looked longingly at the assortment of pastries nestled inside. "I had such a craving, you wouldn't believe."

Kendall cast a guilty glance at the bowl of fresh fruit centered on the breakfast bar. Here she was, doing her utmost to change the eating habits of an entire family, and she knew she was about to conveniently forget her own rules.

"I have a theory about things like this," she said with a very straight face. "Any time a pregnant woman is willing to share her craving, the calories magically disappear." She was sure she'd made a lifelong friend when Leza beamed and waddled over to the paper towel rack.

"Just so you know," Leza said as she plunked down into one of the captain's chairs at the table, "Jared sent me over to grill you about your past."

Oddly, Kendall wasn't surprised, angry, or threatened. In fact, she'd been waiting for something like this. She sat to Leza's left and poured them each a glass of low-fat milk. They both looked at the carton, then the bakery box, and broke into giggles.

"Consider me warned," Kendall finally managed to say around a big bite of the best tasting cinnamon roll she'd had in more years than she cared to think about.

Leza washed down her chocolate-covered doughnut with several short swallows of milk. "Okay, let the inquisition begin." She dabbed at the corners of her lips with a country blue napkin. "Seriously, do you mind? Jared's been beside himself because Jake won't tell him anything other than he found you through your parole officer in Houston.''

Kendall was grateful Jake was leaving it up to her who or who not to tell about her past. If Leza had beat around the bush or tried in any other way to pry the information out of her, Kendall probably would have told her where she could stick her questions. But she liked straight-talking, straight-thinking people. She had a feeling that she and Leza would get along famously.

''You married a smart man, Leza. If he'd come over here today spouting off demands like he did the other day, I'm afraid it wouldn't have been very pleasant.''

Leza toyed with a cinnamon roll that now lay on the paper towel on the table before her. ''I know he came on a little strong, but, Kendall, he was so surprised—'' She stopped in mid-sentence. ''*You* were a surprise. I suppose we just assumed the new housekeeper would be another Esther O'Malley.''

Kendall could understand that and decided to make Leza's mission easier. ''Tell Jared that I got hooked up with a crooked promoter in Houston . . .'' Without going into her personal relationship with Ellis, or even mentioning Courtney, she went on to tell Leza everything, including the district attorney's bloodthirsty tactics and her own attorney's incompetence.

Leza had fallen silent during Kendall's tale. ''You *really* had no idea, did you?'' She looked thoughtful for a long moment after Kendall nodded. ''And he just left you to face the consequences alone?''

Kendall felt her lips curve into a sardonic half-smile. ''Prince Charmings are pretty hard to come by these days.'' Kendall knew before Leza spoke that she'd left herself wide open for what followed.

''I know two,'' Leza said, her quiet conviction about as subtle as a sudden East Texas thunderstorm.

Kendall knew exactly the two she meant. Suddenly she wanted to know everything, anything Leza would be willing to tell her about Jacob Sentell, but she didn't know how to broach the subject.

Leza saved her the effort. "I'll bet you're full of questions about Jake's family."

Kendall put her cinnamon roll aside. "Esther was so busy filling me in on the kids and the house that we never got around to talking about . . ."

"Jake?"

Kendall felt her face flush. "Well," she hedged, "I am living under his roof." Wasn't that as good a reason as any for wanting to know a little background?

Leza didn't even try to hide a knowing smile. "Yes, you are, and I'll be glad to answer any questions you have. Where would you like me to start?"

She could probably get general information out of Jake, but talking about his deceased wife might be a little tricky. "How long were he and Becky married?"

Leza shifted to a more comfortable position in her chair. "I'm a relative newcomer to Rosemont myself. I'd only been here about six months when I met Becky and Jake for the first time. I understand that Becky was his high school sweetheart. They married when he got back from Vietnam and had just celebrated their seventeenth anniversary a few months before she died giving birth to Becca."

Kendall couldn't have been more surprised. No one had ever given her reason to think so, but she'd assumed that Becky had died in an accident of some sort. "But she'd already had four other babies. How could that have happened?"

Leza shrugged. "I honestly don't know. She told me once that she'd been an only child. A very lonely only child. She wanted a houseful of children, which suited

Jake." Her expression sobered. "After Matt's birth, Dr. Lauck advised her not to have more children. She argued with him, and with Jake, but wouldn't agree to have her tubes tied like the doctor wanted. I suppose she hoped her physical condition would get better. And she was just as opposed to Jake having a vasectomy. She convinced him that they could be careful . . ."

Kendall didn't know what to say. She could understand Becky's optimism, but hadn't she understood the risks?

Leza began to fidget with her wedding band. "When she came up pregnant years later, she was thrilled. She wanted to give Jake a little girl more than anything. Jake begged her to follow Dr. Lauck's advice and end the pregnancy, but she wouldn't even consider it. Becky thought it was the answer to her prayers." She grew quiet for a moment before going on. "It was a hard pregnancy, not like the others. She was tired all the time and bedridden toward the end. My housekeeper's cousin—Esther—had just lost her husband and needed work, so Jake hired her to help out. He converted Becky's sewing room into a spare room, and Esther moved in. Things were better for a while, then . . ."

Both women fell silent, and Kendall's mind was awhirl with all she'd just learned. Losing a loved one was always tragic, but this . . .

"Jake was devastated," Leza continued after a moment of silence. "I don't know what would have happened if Esther hadn't been here."

Kendall sensed there was more and wanted, needed, to know. "I can see how much he misses her," she prodded, hoping Leza would go on.

"It was a difficult time for all of us. I was expecting the triplets then, and Jared had his hands full with Jake." Her blue-green eyes clouded with the troubled memories. "I'd never seen Jake take more than a social drink, and suddenly he was drinking heavily, not coming home, sometimes for days on end. It was like he hated anything or anyone who reminded him of what he'd lost. Between Esther, my housekeeper, and myself, the children were cared for, but we were afraid Becky's parents would try to take the children to Fort Worth with them. Thank goodness Jake finally pulled himself together."

Leza had answered many of Kendall's questions, but there were many more she wanted to ask. The telephone rang at that moment, though, and she put her questions aside to answer it.

"Jamison," Jake said unceremoniously, "is Becca up from her nap yet?"

"No, Sheriff, she's still resting." If he insisted on calling her Jamison, she would continue to call him Sheriff.

"Oh," he said, "I have a few hours free this afternoon. Thought I'd spend some time with her." Even over the phone, his voice sounded strained and there was an awkward pause. "I haven't seen much of her in the past few days."

She heard the self-recrimination in his tone, and immediately wanted to do or say something to put his mind at ease. "She should be waking up any time now. I promised to take her horseback riding later, but I'm sure she'd rather go with you."

Another pause. "Why don't we make it a threesome?"

Kendall could tell from Leza's expression that her own was one of pure surprise. "That . . . sounds like fun."

"Good." He sounded more lighthearted. "I'll be home in twenty minutes."

Kendall hung up and turned to find Leza hauling herself out of the chair.

"Looks like you have a date," the pregnant woman said. "I think I'll keep this to myself. Give Jared a little more time to get used to the idea that there's another woman in Jake's life."

"Leza," Kendall admonished, trying her best to sound sincere when secretly she was a mass of nerves inside. "He's coming home to spend some time with Becca." Maybe if she convinced Leza, she'd believe it herself. "He's been working long hours lately—"

"I know all about his long hours," Leza interrupted, reaching the back door. "I'm glad he's finally got something other than the kids to come home to."

Kendall stood staring at the door for a long few seconds after Leza and her pastry box were gone. Things were moving way too fast to suit her. The attraction she'd felt from the very first moment she laid eyes on Jake Sentell had been a force to be reckoned with, but to have others aware of it was unsettling as hell. She'd have to do something to rectify Leza's misconception about Jake's interest in her. In the meantime—

Time! She glanced at the clock, then down at her perspiration-soaked sweats. He would be home in less than twenty minutes.

The kitchen was empty, but the door to Jamison's room was open. Glancing inside, Jake saw that her bedroom furniture had been delivered and set up. From the sound of water running in her bathroom, he gathered that she'd already moved her belongings downstairs.

She amazed him. In the four days that Esther had been gone, Jamison had his home running as efficiently as the older woman ever had. And she'd made major changes so subtly that the children were hardly aware of them. Although he hadn't been home at mealtime, Josh had told him that they were eating together at the table instead of in front of the television and that their homework had to be done and checked before anyone got to watch TV or go out to play. Josh was coming around, which, he was sure, made Timmy and Matt easier to deal with.

He smiled, something he found he was doing more and more often. Things just might work out, after all. He'd had his doubts, especially after Sunday, but if he could just keep his thoughts and his hands to himself, he was sure everything would work out fine. Which led him right back to the reason he'd invited her to spend the afternoon with him and Becca—to prove to himself that they could be together without groping each other.

The water stopped running, and a mental image of Kendall—Jamison—no, Kendall—stepping out of the shower and wrapping a thick, fluffy towel around her tall, perfectly proportioned body popped into his brain. . . .

The steady hum of a blow-dryer brought him back to his senses, and with a self-disparaging oath, he headed for the stairs. Hell, he never thought it was going to be easy.

Returning several minutes later, he again found the bedroom door open. This time, Jamison sat at the dresser, fully dressed and brushing her hair, apparently unaware of his presence. He watched, transfixed, with Becca's sleepy head snuggled between his shoulder and his jaw, as Kendall pulled one of three separated sections of glossy, strawberry-blond hair over the other two, then repeated the process from the other side. How she accomplished the task of a perfectly straight French braid down her back without a third hand was a mystery to him. But, then, everything about her was a mystery, a mystery he found himself wanting to unravel.

He hadn't made a sound, but he saw her hands still, felt his breath get lost somewhere in his throat when she turned to see him watching her. There was no embarrassment, no words or looks of reproach from her; she simply tied off the end of the braid and stood. Today she wore a new shirt, or rather a blouse, of soft yellow cotton tucked inside a pair of faded jeans.

"When did you get home?" she asked, gently rubbing Becca's back. She stood close enough now that she caught the scent of an intoxicating fragrance. He'd noticed several new items of clothing since he'd given her her first paycheck. And now perfume. Was she bent on driving him crazy?

"A little while ago." He wanted to put his hand over hers, anything to make physical contact. But he didn't. "Hope you don't mind that I went ahead and got her up."

The smile that eased across her lips—such kissable lips—made him ache a little inside. "She's your child, Sheriff."

"Jake," he said, realizing suddenly that although he'd told her to call him Jake, she'd never done so. And just as suddenly, he wanted to hear her say his name.

"I see you've changed clothes, but have you eaten?" she asked without acknowledging his correction.

"Yeah." *But I'm hungry for you.* This was crazy. Why was he thinking this way?

Gently taking Becca from him, she gathered a pair of socks and shoes from the breakfast bar and sat down to put them on her.

"All done," she said, standing and smoothing Becca's hair. "Your daddy's taking you riding instead of me."

"I thought you wanted to come along."

"I did," she answered, lowering her gaze. "But this way I can get supper started early for a change."

Before Jake could argue, Becca took Kendall by the hand. "My want you to go, too, Kenny. Pwease."

"Come on, Jamison," Jake said. "A break'll do you good." Until she said she wasn't coming along, he hadn't realized how much he'd been looking forward to her accompanying them on their ride.

He watched her looking down at Becca and knew that she wanted to go just as badly. Was he the reason she was hedging?

"I haven't forgotten my promise from Sunday morning, if that's what's bothering you," he told her, guessing at the reason she was reluctant to accept his invitation. He hoped she believed him. "I'll even help with supper after we get back."

She raised her gaze to meet his and smiled. "You talked me into it," she said after the briefest of pauses. "There's something I need to talk to with you about when we get back, though. Remind me, okay?"

Jake nodded, unable to believe how happy he was that she had agreed to go along. Since when did he want to spend every free moment with her?

Kendall hadn't been in the saddle for at least five years, longer than that if she thought back on it. The mare Jake had chosen for her was gentle and responsive, though, and she fell back into riding as if she'd been doing it every day of her life. And she was having the time of her life, enjoying the scenery and Jake's and Becca's descriptions of their favorite picnic spot.

Reaching Twin Oaks on Cold Creek, Jake dismounted, then helped Becca to the ground. Kendall didn't wait for the hand she knew would be there to help her down. Instead, she quickly dismounted, then tethered the mare herself.

"We'll take a short break before heading back," Jake told her, watching Becca dash off after a large, brightly colored monarch butterfly. Kendall joined him in laughter as they watched the child chasing the elusive insect.

During the leisurely ride to Twin Oaks, Kendall had listened to Becca and Jake talk about their favorite campsite and how they would pack up their camping gear soon for the first overnight trip of the summer. Now she could see how the place could be a favorite, with two sprawling live oaks standing some twenty feet apart, their long branches dipping low to the ground. One long limb swooped out over the creek, and she saw a rope swing dangling above the water. What a perfect place for a family outing.

Then she turned her attention to the acres of pastureland surrounding them. For as far as the eye could see, there were rolling hills dotted with oak and hickory trees. In the distance a herd of solid white cattle meandered toward the horizon.

"I don't think I've ever seen cows like those," she observed aloud.

"Charolais," Jake told her. "Jared and I brought them in several years ago. They're doing great."

"You and your brother ranch together?"

"Among other things," he answered, taking the time to sit down on the ground.

"Such as?" she prompted.

He stretched out in the grass and crossed his booted ankles. "Oil, brick plants, and the rose farms. And, of course, there are the cattle." He looked at her. "Our property lines adjoin, making Summerset and Cold Creek the largest ranch in this part of the state—'' He stopped and gave her a perfectly charming, sheepish grin. ''Sounds a lot like bragging to me.''

''No, not at all. I asked, remember.'' That cleared up a lot of things in Kendall's mind. She'd often wondered how he could afford the lifestyle he provided for his family on a sheriff's salary.

''So,'' she said, taking a seat beside him under one of the live oaks that hugged the edge of the creek, ''how long have you been the sheriff around here?''

Jake broke off a blade of St. Augustine grass and slipped it between his lips. ''I ran for office twelve years ago. Been sheriff ever since.'' He sat up and called, ''Becca, don't go any farther.'' The child obeyed immediately, then he relaxed, stretched out on his back in the grass, and continued to play with the blade of grass between his lips.

She watched those lips with more interest than she wanted to admit, felt her own tongue slip out and moisten her lips when his did the same.

''Were you always interested in the law?'' she asked, more to distract her own wayward thoughts at this point than anything else.

''I suppose,'' he said absently. ''But it wasn't until Vietnam when they made me an MP that I thought about it seriously.'' He rolled to one side, bent his elbow, and rested his head on the heel of his hand. ''A couple of years after Jared and I got back from 'Nam, we bought a two-truck swabbing outfit and really got our feet wet in the oil business.'' He laughed, apparently remembering. ''Boy, we were green back then. Our old man had been a roughneck, and we'd worked the oil patch some, so we thought we'd hit something big when we ran across Marshall Houston wanting to sell one of his businesses. What we didn't know was that we needed at least four other men to work the trucks efficiently. But we learned the hard way and in the end it all paid off." He chuckled again, and Kendall found herself wanting to know more.

"So what happened next?"

He cut his pewter-gray eyes at her. "You really interested in all this?"

No one had ever made Kendall feel that he could see straight into her soul before. "Yes, of course, I'm interested."

Taking a second to check on Becca again, Jake resumed his tale. "By this time Becky was expecting Brad, and I knew I had to find something more stable than the oil field to put the bacon on the table. I made it through the academy, hired on as a deputy, advanced through the ranks, then decided that I would make a damn good sheriff." He said it with pride, and Kendall knew that he *was* a damn good sheriff.

It was one of the few times he'd ever mentioned Becky, and Kendall knew it was a good sign that he'd done so without the pained expression that usually accompanied thoughts of his dead wife. Progress.

"You mentioned your father; do your folks live around here?" For the briefest of moments she thought she saw a flicker of another kind of pain, one that was older, yet still there.

"Dad died a couple of years after my mother deserted us," he said simply. "Drank himself into an early grave."

Boy, did that hit home with her. They had so much in common—both had been deserted by a parent, then lived with an alcoholic parent, although hers had been a stepfather. "I'm sorry." She heard her voice quaver.

"Hey," he said, leaning forward to cup her chin in his palm. "It's all right. It's in the past."

Unintentionally he'd opened an old wound for her, and she couldn't respond, not even to his touch. Although she often wondered why her father had left and whether or not he was alive and well, it wasn't something she ever wanted to talk about.

"I have a feeling we just dredged up something unpleasant." He lowered his hand.

He'd been nothing but honest with her. The least she could do was share with him. She gave him a wan smile. "It's just that my father walked out on my mom and me when I was ten. It was hard for us to make a go of it until she met my stepfather . . ."

She hadn't meant to tell him about Randall Blankenship, Courtney's father, and was stunned that she'd ventured so close to a relationship she had valiantly tried to conceal for years.

"Stepfather?" he said thoughtfully. "Was it that bad?"

"Well, yes and no." How could she explain life with an alcoholic stepfather who was out of work more often than not without sounding self-pitying? "It wasn't ideal, but Momma really had no other choice. We had a roof over our heads and we didn't go hungry. Then Momma died . . ." Guilt reared its ugly head. Would she ever be able to think about her mother without remembering her promise to watch out for Courtney?

Enough about her, she decided, coming to her feet and looking at the sky. "Becca," she called, noticing that Jake had also stood up. "It looks like rain. We'd better head back to the house. Do you want to ride with me or your dad?"

"Daddy," Becca squealed, her short little legs closing the distance between them faster than Kendall thought possible. She bounded into her father's waiting arms, laughing when he nuzzled her neck with a growling bear hug.

More than anything, Kendall wanted to join in, be a part of such a spontaneous show of affection. But she wasn't a part of this family. Would she ever be this important to anyone?

Sensing Jake's gaze on her, she pushed back a lock of hair that had fallen across her brow. The stark emotion she saw reflected in his eyes made her insides turn to gelatin.

"Thanks for today," he said simply.

She met his silver-gray gaze. "I should thank you. Today was one of the best days I've had in . . . a long, long time."

This time she let him give her a hand up into the saddle, and listening to Becca's incessant chatter, she smiled most of the way back to the house.

No sooner had they unsaddled and tended the horses than Kendall heard Timmy call from outside, "Where is everybody?"

She and Becca followed Jake out of the barn to see Timmy and Matt descending the back porch steps. Close on their heels trotted a skinny black dog, her milk-laden teats hanging dangerously close to the ground. Kendall's heart immediately went out to both the dog and the boys: to the dog because skinny was an inadequate description for what she suspected was a stray, a grossly undernourished and obviously nursing female stray; to the boys because it was apparent that they had no idea of what they had done. One look at Jake and she knew that it was only a matter of minutes before they would be enlightened.

"Hi, Dad," Timmy called to them. "The bus broke down at our turnoff and we walked home. We already

called the bus barn to let them know what happened.''
He went down on one knee to wrap his arm around the
dog's neck. "She followed us all the way from the
roadside park,'' he said, and Kendall had no problem
imagining the amount of coaxing the poor animal had
endured during the half-mile walk.

"Yeah," Matt chimed in, "she was sniffing 'round
the trash cans looking for food. I gave her the scraps
out of my lunch box," he added, a pleased-with-him-
self smile turning up the corners of his lips.

She saw by the expression on Jake's face that he was
dreading the task of reprimanding his sons for their
good deed gone wrong. But there was a litter of puppies
out there somewhere, probably near the roadside park,
waiting for their mother to return.

Becca broke free from Kendall's grasp and raced
toward the dog. "Oh, Daddy," she cried, "can we
keep her?"

Kendall managed to relieve the dog of Becca's embrace. "I'll take Becca inside while you explain," she
told Jake. It would be easier for him to convince the
boys to take the dog back without Becca's pleading
eyes testing his resolve.

"But, Dad," she heard Matt whine a moment later
as she stood at the back door, "why can't we just keep
her?"

"Didn't you hear me, son?" A note of exasperation
edged Jake's voice. "If we don't get her back to the
park so she can find and nurse her puppies, they'll
die."

Kendall knew it had to be difficult for Jake to be so
blunt, but those were the hard, cruel facts. Both boys'
heads drooped. Neither said another word for several
long seconds.

Finally Timmy raised his gaze to meet Jake's. "We didn't mean to hurt nobody." His voice cracked.

"I know that, son."

Timmy stroked the dog's head, then stood. "C'mon, Matt. It'll be dark soon. Let's take her back."

"Put her in the back of the pickup," Jake said, glancing skyward. "Looks like a storm's brewing." He looked at Kendall. "We'll be home in time for supper."

She'd known all along that he wouldn't let Timmy and Matt do the deed alone, but she couldn't resist teasing him to ease the mood. "I knew you'd find a way to get out of helping with dinner."

Jake returned her smile, then followed his sons to the truck parked near the barn. She watched them go, laughing when thunder rumbled and rain poured from the gray Texas sky, forcing them to sprint for the truck.

Later, while Becca helped with supper, Kendall glanced repeatedly out the window and at the clock. Josh was due home any time now; Jake and the boys had been gone well over an hour. And the storm was growing steadily worse. Her worry grew by the minute and she was thinking about going to check on them when she saw headlights flash across the backyard. Then she heard Timmy and Matt outside the door, wiping their feet.

Anxious to know why they were so late, she went to the door to meet them. "Where's your father?" she asked, seeing that they were alone.

"He's putting Bob in the barn."

"Bob?" Kendall hadn't the faintest idea who Bob was or why Jake would be putting him in the barn.

"The dog," Timmy explained, giving up on wiping his shoes clean on the doormat. He took them off and left them beside Matt's outside the door. "She's so skinny that Matt and me was calling her Bag of Bones. Dad said that wasn't very nice, so we shortened it to Bob.'' He and Matt automatically gathered plates, glasses, and flatware and began to set the table while they talked.

"Anyway," Timmy went on, "Dad says we can keep Bob, but we'll have to find good homes for the puppies once they're old enough."

"I see," Kendall said, not at all surprised that the dog had taken up residence at Cold Creek Ranch. "But why did it take so long?"

Timmy and Matt looked at each other and started to laugh.

"Well," Timmy said, sitting at the breakfast bar while Kendall checked the roast one last time, "when we got to the park, Bob just stood there in the rain. She looked like she didn't know what was going on."

"Yeah," Matt said with his head inside the refrigerator door. Turning, he poured himself a glass of milk. "And Dad looked real worried. He said she was a young dog and that this was probably her first litter. He couldn't just leave and hope she'd go back to her pups, so we waited. After twenty or thirty minutes, she wandered off and Dad decided to follow her." He took a sip of his milk and Timmy took over again.

"It was raining real hard by then, and . . ." Again he and Matt looked at each other, this time laughing so hard that Kendall barely made out the "and he fell in the creek" that they said at the same time.

"You two still think it's funny?"

No one had heard Jake come in. Kendall looked up and the sight she saw standing in the doorway made it impossible to keep a straight face. Soaked to the skin, he was covered with mud and grass, and the brim of his perfectly handsome straw Resistol dipped limply over his forehead and eyes.

It took everything in her to keep from laughing. "Are you okay?"

"Do I look okay?" What should have been a grumpy retort came out with a grin that left everyone laughing, including Jake.

"What's going on?" Josh stood behind Jake, his athletic bag in his hand, a confused expression on his face. In a matter of minutes Matt and Timmy filled Josh in on the events of the afternoon. Shaking his head at his father, Josh wandered off to the den, the boys and Becca following him.

Alone, Jake and Kendall finally pulled themselves together long enough for Jake to say, "I don't want to track this all over the house. Do you mind if I shower and change in your bathroom?" He'd already stepped out of his boots outside, but his clothes were a soggy, muddy mess.

"Of course not. My robe's in the laundry room. Get out of your grubby things in there while I get you a fresh set of clothes from upstairs."

Returning to her room moments later with clean underwear, jeans, and a shirt, she pulled up short at the foot of her bed. The door to her bathroom stood slightly ajar, and Jake's full torso was reflected in the mirror. She had a clear view of him. Her blue robe fit tight across his wide shoulders, hiking it up to where the hem struck him mid-calf. Never had she dreamed that the terry cloth garment could look so silly, yet sexy. No sooner had that thought cleared than the robe in question slid off his shoulders to puddle around his bare feet.

Quickly glancing toward the kitchen, she knew she should leave. She didn't want to take the chance of one of the children catching her gaping at Jake like a common Peeping Tom. But she didn't go. His bare bottom and broad shoulders were like a magnet pulling her gaze back for one last longing look. His arms were muscular and well defined. His thighs looked rock-hard and strong.

She closed her eyes and could almost feel the warmth of his hands on her skin, rough and callused, yet gentle in unhurried exploration. A quiver of desire coursed through her. When she opened her eyes, Jake's gaze was on her. Facing her now, he was as unembarrassed as she as her gaze continued its perusal of his well-developed torso, across the breadth of his shoulders and chest, down the tapering length and flat contour of his abdomen . . . then lower.

"Kenny," Becca called, causing Kendall to jump at the sound. Jake smiled then and stepped into her shower.

"I'll be right there," Kendall answered, praying that her face wasn't as flushed with color as her body was with desire.

SEVEN

No mention was made that evening regarding her glimpse of Jake in her bathroom. Her biggest problem with the incident was her reaction to the sight of his perfectly perfect body. Although sex with Ellis had never been unpleasant, neither had it been the rapturous experience she'd read about or dreamed it would be. Something told her that wouldn't be the case with Jake Sentell.

The man oozed virility and sexuality, and he constantly surprised Kendall by being a man of contradictions. At work she was sure he was rough and tough, macho, as it were, able to deal with criminals on their level and on a daily basis. She'd glimpsed his tender side before, mostly with his children, but tonight he'd proved it all over again in such a way that it was impossible to deny. How many men would follow a skinny mama dog through a stormy night to find a passel of puppies someone else obviously hadn't wanted and had discarded without conscience? She smiled at the image of him falling in the creek, coming out wet and grumpy and carrying an armful of puppies back to his truck. The next image that flashed through her mind wasn't so innocent; neither was it one she could easily banish. His smile just before he stepped into her shower hadn't been mocking or seductive. *Understanding* was more like it. He'd known how he affected her, and it had pleased him.

Stop it, she commanded herself, quickly forcing her mind to the task of overseeing the cleanup of the kitchen after dinner. She couldn't continue this train of thought and be able to look him in the eye, and she needed to tell him about her discovery earlier today.

After asking Josh to keep an eye on things while she had a moment with Jake in his study, she straightened her blouse as well as her spine and knocked on his door. No sense putting it off any longer. They had a problem that wouldn't go away without intervention on Jake's part.

"Do you have a minute?" she asked, sliding the door closed behind her.

Jake looked up from the papers on his desk. "Yes, of course. You said earlier you had something to discuss with me. Is it that serious?" he asked, obviously referring to her frown.

"Sort of depends on your reaction." She approached his desk and placed a stack of magazines in front of him. "I found these this morning."

He picked up the top magazine and his expression tightened. Flipping through the pages, he held it up and the centerfold flopped out right in his face. One dark eyebrow rose in male appreciation. Finally he looked up. "Where?"

Kendall looked him squarely in the eye. "I had to turn your mattress, and there they were."

His expression was priceless. "These aren't mine."

Kendall suppressed a smile. "I never thought they were."

Now he looked confused.

"Sheriff," she began, "if you had something you didn't want your father to find, where would be the last place you'd expect him to look?"

Comprehension dawned on him. "What safer place than the father's room, under his mattress?" He came to his feet. "Any idea which boy we're talking about here?"

Kendall shook her head. "Since they were in your room, your guess is as good as mine." She turned to go, then stopped to face him again. This time she didn't try to conceal her amusement. "You could always brush them for fingerprints," she said with a giggle.

Later, after Becca was down for the night, Jake called a family meeting in his study. Kendall was glad he wasn't one to put off things, unpleasant or otherwise. Obviously he wanted to get to the bottom of who had hidden the magazines between his mattress and box springs. And, he told Kendall, he wanted her there because now was as good a time as any for the boys to know the truth about her past.

All three boys stood before Jake's desk, each of them looking uneasy under his father's somber visage. Kendall had taken the wing chair to Jake's left. A fire blazed in the fireplace, adding a touch of warmth the early spring night needed.

"There are two things we need to talk about tonight," Jake began. "First, I have something in my desk that's been hidden under my mattress." He didn't say who had found the "something," and Kendall suspected it was his way of saving everyone any more embarrassment. He paused to let his words sink in, and

Kendall saw his gaze move from boy to boy to boy. "This is something that needs to be dealt with in private," he said with a pointed look at Kendall. "One of you knows what I'm referring to, and I expect you to come to me later tonight." Three pairs of eyes looked at the floor, and no one said a word. The only sounds Kendall heard were the crackle of the fire and the ticking of the grandfather clock in the entry hallway.

"Now," Jake said, taking a seat in the swivel chair behind his desk, "Esther's been gone almost a week, and I need to know how each of you feels about the job Jamison's doing." Now that their father wasn't towering over them any longer the boys visibly relaxed. One by one, their attention shifted to Kendall. Jake had put them on the spot, but she assumed he knew his sons well enough to know what he was doing.

"Well, Josh, is she working out?"

Josh swallowed: Hard. "Dad, I don't think it's fair to compare Kendall to Esther so soon."

"I didn't mean to do that, son," Jake answered. "It's just that I'm not here during the day and thought that if you had any gripes, it would be better to handle them now instead of later."

Josh threw a worried glance at Kendall. "She does a lot of things different than Esther, but . . . I think she's doing okay."

High praise, indeed, coming from someone who just four short days ago resented having to help clear away the dishes.

"Yeah," Matt hurried to add, "and she's been helping me with my photography class and my karate exercises." His eyes blinked rapidly, then came to rest on his father. "Esther couldn't do that."

A smile tugged at Kendall's lips. Matthew had never

given her one moment's grief, unless it had been at Timmy's prodding, and she was touched by his eagerness to come to her defense. She felt her chest tighten. Josh and Matt had accepted her. For reasons she didn't understand, she wanted to laugh; she wanted to cry. But that would be premature. Timmy was going to be the hard one.

"Timmy?" Jake asked.

Timmy didn't say anything for a few long seconds. "I got no complaints," he finally said.

Kendall saw Jake try not to smile. "No complaints?" He waited, the pause forcing Timmy to look up at him. "That's not quite good enough, son."

The middle boy glanced from his father to Kendall, then back at his shoes. "I don't like having to make my bed every morning or all the fruit she makes us eat instead of cookies and stuff," he started. "But she helped me understand what Mr. Haskins wanted me to do with my science project."

Jake gave Kendall a victory wink. "So you're all in agreement that she's doing a good job?" They all looked relieved and nodded, even Timmy. "And you're happy with her in our home?" Again three heads nodded their agreement.

"Good. It's settled. That is, if Jamison doesn't have any gripes against us." He left the floor open to her.

Kendall was still trying to gather her composure over everyone's acceptance of her and found it difficult to speak around the lump in her throat. "I'm perfectly happy, Sheriff," she managed to say.

Jake gave her a smile of encouragement. "Do you want to take it from here, or do you want me to tell them?"

Until this very moment, she hadn't realized just how important the boys' reaction to learning of her past indiscretion could be. Would they understand, and, more important, would they still want her to stay? Or would they be too uncomfortable with a jailbird living in their home?

She clasped her hands in her lap. What would be, would be, she decided with a resigned straightening of her shoulders. "I'm not proud of what I have to tell you." From the corner of her eye, she saw Jake settle back in his chair. She cleared her throat and continued. "Several years ago I got into some trouble with the law down in Houston."

Shock registered on each boy's face. She had their undivided attention.

"I spent some time in prison paying for that mistake and hope I can put it behind me and go on with my life."

"You were in jail?" Matt asked, his wonderful hazel eyes wide with disbelief and curiosity. "What did you do?"

Kendall didn't want to lie to them, but she couldn't tell the whole story without doing so. Without thinking, she looked to Jake for help.

He took over without a moment's hesitation. "She worked for a man she didn't know was a scam artist. He swindled thousands of dollars from a lot of people who trusted him, then he skipped town." He leaned forward, lacing his fingers together. "When she couldn't tell the police where to find him, she was charged, tried, and convicted of fraud. All she did wrong was trust someone she cared for."

A knot the size of a Buick formed in the pit of her stomach. There was no way Jake could know about her relationship with Ellis, but somehow he'd gotten his facts straight.

"I learned a hard lesson the hard way," she managed to say, her voice soft and low.

Jake waited for everything he and Kendall had told them to sink in, then he stood. "Well, boys, what do you say?" For one long, awkward moment of silence, the ticking of the clock and the crackle of the fire filled the cozy room.

Kendall held her breath, waiting. Then Josh looked straight at her. "Everyone makes mistakes, Dad," he said, giving Kendall the impression that he was talking from experience. "I think we'll keep her."

"Yeah," Timmy and Matt chimed in at the same time.

Kendall felt tears stinging her eyes. Jake and his sons were all looking at her expectantly, and she still couldn't say a word.

Josh broke the awkward silence. "Dad, I need to talk with you in private."

So Josh was the culprit with an eye for the scantily clad ladies. Kendall saw the pride in Jake's eyes that his son was man enough to speak up and accept the consequences for his actions.

Timmy cleared his throat with a nervous cough. "I guess you'd better make time for me after Josh," he said, so softly that everyone did a quick double take at him.

She and Jake exchanged stunned looks.

Matt shifted from one foot to the other. "Me, too, Dad," he said, not quite as loudly as Josh or Timmy, but just as guiltily.

"I'll be damned," Jake said with a shake of his head. "All three of you?" He threaded his fingers through his dark hair. "I've heard of hand-me-down's, but *this* takes the cake." Then, to Kendall, he said, "If you'll excuse us, Jamison, my sons and I have some serious talking to do.''

Jake had known he was taking a chance by asking the boys about Kendall with her in the same room. But he also knew that if he could get them to admit they thought she was doing a good job and wanted her to stay, they'd be more receptive to the truth about her past.

Still, what he didn't know was why he had come to her rescue when Matt asked her why she'd been in jail. He knew she wouldn't have lied to them, and he'd have finally learned why she'd taken the heat for the Houston scam.

Because, he argued with himself, staring at the charred remains of the nudie magazines lying in the fireplace, he didn't want her forced to share her private life with him. He wanted, needed, her to trust him enough to tell him the whole truth.

Their time together this afternoon had proved what he'd hoped it would: He could be with her, even touch her, and not feel out of control. Or had it been easy because Becca was with them? If that was the case, they were right back to square one and all his ideas about self-control were a lot of bull.

After their talk today at Cold Creek, he knew a little more about her. Which made him feel better about a lot of things, especially since the trouble she'd gotten into in Houston was driving him crazy. Maybe it was the lawman in him, but he was determined to unravel the mystery surrounding one Kendall Leigh Jamison.

And, slowly but surely, he was doing just that. From the first time he'd read her file, he'd had a gut feeling that there was more behind her reasons for not speaking out against Trammell and Blankenship at her trial than simply not knowing where they'd gone. His conversations with her parole officer had only reinforced that feeling. Nancy Bigelow had sounded as if she wanted to tell him more on the phone that day. Still, he'd known at the time that she had steered the conversation away from Trammell and especially Blankenship. Why?

From down the hall, he heard Becca giggle over something Kendall said, and he smiled. Suddenly he remembered Becca mentioning that Kendall's sister hadn't been able to say her name either. Why hadn't he picked up on that piece of the puzzle at the time? Her file listed no next of kin, so why had she mentioned a sister to Becca? Was that the connection between her and Blankenship?

Maybe because his mind was working so furiously to figure it all out, he remembered something Kendall had told him this afternoon, something, he suspected, she hadn't meant to reveal. She'd had a stepfather, which led to the logical conclusion, or at least logical to someone looking for answers, that Courtney Blankenship could be Kendall Jamison's sister. Or stepsister. And if Blankenship had been involved with Trammell, too . . . That just might explain Kendall's reasons for protecting the two of them, even at her own expense.

Although he'd alluded to the fact earlier with the boys, he still wasn't sure if there had been something personal between Kendall and Trammell, but at least now some of it made sense. If Kendall had tried to clear herself by telling the truth, the law might have been able to gather enough information to track Trammell down, finding Blankenship in the process. It was a chance Kendall obviously hadn't been willing to take.

Jake admired loyalty in a person, but, dammit, she'd taken it to the extreme—and lost some of the best years of her life.

* * *

The days turned into weeks and March into April, with Kendall giving hardly any thought to how busy she was. They fell into an easy routine that was agreeable to everyone. Each school morning, Kendall was up no later than six, making lunches and cooking breakfast while the boys dressed, made their beds, and brought their laundry down to the utility room. Then they were off to feed Bob and play with the pups for a few minutes before breakfast. Jake woke Becca and helped her dress. Then everyone met in the kitchen for a few minutes of early morning camaraderie before the boys caught the school bus and Jake left for work. Jake even managed to come home for lunch with Becca from time to time, especially on those days he knew he'd be working late.

"My don't wike cauwifwower," Becca insisted, eyeing the steamed vegetable on the plate before her.

"*I* don't like cauliflower," Kendall gently corrected. She'd been working on Becca's speech patterns and, for the most part, it showed. She'd never had a real problem saying her *r*'s, but *l*'s still gave her trouble. And her habit of saying *my* instead of *I* was going to be a hard one to break.

Becca looked across the table, her eyes wide and innocent. "If you don't wike it and my don't wike it, why we gotta eat it?"

Kendall heard Jake chuckle and shot him a look that made him shrug a silent apology, stab his own cauliflower, and pop it into his mouth.

The jangle of the telephone kept her from insisting that Becca at least try the scorned vegetable.

"Hello," she said. There was a pause on the other end of the line. "Sentell residence."

"Oh, hello," a decidedly male voice finally said. "You must be Kendall."

Kendall tucked the earpiece snugly between her shoulder and ear while motioning for Becca to eat. "Yes?"

"This is Brad. I called the office. They said Dad was home for lunch."

"Yes, he is. Sheriff—"

"Wait, Kendall," Brad said, cutting her off. "I just called to let Dad know I'll be home this weekend, but while I have you . . ." He paused, his silence piquing Kendall's interest. "Saturday is Becca's birthday. Since she's never had a party before, do you suppose we could do something special?"

Jake had approached her while Brad talked, and he stood next to her now. "Sure," she said, switching ears with the receiver. "No one told me, but I'll be glad to arrange something. Just the family?"

"Yeah, that sounds good. And, Kendall, don't let Dad talk you out of it."

Kendall wasn't sure what to say to that. Why would Jake object to his daughter's having a birthday party? "It was good talking to you, Brad," she said, deciding not to question his cryptic remark now. "Your dad's right here."

"Can't wait to meet you in person, Kendall. See you Friday evening."

Jake took the telephone and greeted his son. Kendall joined Becca at the table, wondering at Brad's revelation that Becca had never had a birthday party. If he was afraid that his father would object, would he tell Jake that he'd asked her to plan a party, or would he let her tell him?

"Okay, son. See you Friday. Drive carefully." Jake

hung up, smiling. "It'll be good to see Brad. He hasn't been home since Christmas."

"Brad's comin' home?" Becca's eyes sparkled.

"Yes, Snuggle Bug, and he asked me to give you a big hug." He took her in his arms and gave her the promised squeeze.

Kendall watched with a growing sense of unease as it dawned on her that Becca's birthday was the same day Becky had died. That was why Brad had been so ambiguous, why Jake might object.

She watched Jake tweak Becca's nose and they both laughed. Obviously, Brad hadn't mentioned the birthday party. "He sounds like a fine young man," she said, knowing now that it would be best to ease into the topic of the party. "Not very many older brothers would remember a baby sister's birthday." She saw Jake's shoulders stiffen as he settled Becca back in her chair. "He asked me to plan a family celebration for Saturday." Brad had put her in a difficult position, but Becca deserved a party. And maybe by facing it head on, Jake would be better able to deal with his own emotions. "Do you want to call Jared and Leza, or do you want me to handle it?"

"My gonna have a birthday?" Becca's question drew her father's attention away from Kendall.

"You call them," Jake said, his terse tone of voice clearly puzzling Becca. "I have to get back to work." With that, he took his hat from the peg by the back door and was gone.

"What's wrong with Daddy?"

Kendall looked down at the child. "Nothing, sweetheart," she answered. "Would you like to help clear away the dishes?"

"Sure."

Watching Becca take her plate, uneaten cauliflower

and all, to the sink, Kendall realized how hard it was going to be for Jake to celebrate the child's birthday. She would do her best to make it as painless as possible, but life went on, and Becca was going to have the best birthday any three-year-old had ever had. Already Kendall was making plans. A late afternoon get-together—perhaps a barbecue—with presents and games would be fun for everyone, especially Becca and the triplets. She'd ask Leza if there were other youngsters she could invite, and she'd include Becca in everything, from buying the decorations to baking and decorating the cake. This would be fun.

Then she remembered Jake's solemn expression, and she wondered at how much fun it would be after all.

Jake couldn't believe he'd been so hard to live with the past few days. Ever since Brad's call at the beginning of the week, he'd been surly and just plain ornery. No one at home or the office had been spared his foul mood, not even Becca. He'd snapped at her several times, something he never did. Even though he hated himself for it, he didn't seem capable of controlling his temper—especially when he came home every night to find more evidence of the impending celebration.

Sitting behind closed doors in his study, he listened to the nightly ritual of his children preparing for bed. He turned up the glass, realizing that the bourbon didn't burn anymore on its way down. How many drinks did this make? Two? Three? Not enough to blot out the anger that no one—not one of his sons, neither Jared nor Leza—*no one* seemed to remember that tomorrow Becky would be gone three long years.

This time, the bourbon tasted bitter on his tongue. Self-pity was no more his style than was ignoring the needs of his daughter. Although Becky had died giving birth, he'd never blamed Becca. Why should he? She hadn't asked to be born, after all. Besides, he knew exactly where to lay the blame, and that was what was so hard to live with. And he also had to admit that he had never even bought Becca a birthday gift, much less planned a party for her. Before, when the date rolled around each year, it hadn't seemed all that important. But she was old enough now to know what she was missing. It wasn't fair for her to miss out on something so special simply because her birthday and the anniversary of her mother's death fell on the same day.

The glass clutched in his hand was nearly full, and he set it aside with a scowl aimed at no one but himself. Drinking had never been the answer. It was just easy. The pain, dulled for a few brief hours, always came back. No matter how difficult, he'd put aside his own feelings and go out tomorrow and buy his daughter the cutest baby doll he could find.

He scrubbed his hand over his face and tried to clear his thoughts. Brad should be rolling in any minute now, and he still had the Story-That-Never-Ends to get through. He wanted to have a clear head for both.

Kendall had just put the last of the supper dishes in the dishwasher when she heard a car pull into the driveway behind the house. Becca and Jake were in his study, but Josh, Timmy, and Matt heard it, too. They raced from the den, through the kitchen, and out the door before Kendall could take off her apron. From the shouts she heard, she knew Brad had made it in from Austin. Jake and Becca must have heard the commotion because they entered the kitchen at the exact time the four rowdy boys roughhoused through the back door.

"Brad!" Becca squealed, deserting Jake to bound

into her oldest brother's waiting arms. "I'm glad you're home. We're gonna have a birthcake party tomorrow."

Kendall had tried in vain to convince Becca that it was a *birthday* party, but ever since they'd bought the ingredients for the cake, it had become a *birthcake* party.

Brad laughed and swung her into his arms. "Whoa, Snuggle Bug. What's this I heard. *L*'s and *r*'s and *I* instead of *my*?"

Becca puffed up with pride. "Kenny's helping me talk like a big girl," she jabbered on. "I'm three years old, you know."

Everyone laughed, but it was Jake who spoke next. "Glad you're home, son." They embraced each other, then broke apart with good-natured jibes.

Kendall had seen photographs of Brad, but none had done him justice. Brad Sentell lacked an inch or so reaching his father's height of over six feet, but once he matured, he'd be blessed with the same rugged good looks and lean, muscular physique as his father. With the exception of his sandy hair, he was the spitting image of Jake.

"And," Brad said, glancing past Jake, "this must be Kendall." He gave her an appreciative once-over. "Josh said you were gorgeous. Can't fault his eyesight."

Josh's face turned the color of a Texas sunset as Kendall said a polite thank you.

"Are you hungry?" she asked. "I just put the supper leftovers away, but they should still be warm."

"No, thanks. I grabbed a burger a few miles back." Then to Josh, he said, "Help me get my things out of my car. I brought everybody something." That's all it took to get everyone out of the kitchen.

The glow of contentment Kendall felt as she watched them leave was something she was intensely aware of.

And it almost hurt. She looked up to find Jake watching her.

"You're a lucky man, Jake Sentell."

He smiled and, like a camera, her mind took a picture of him that would be with her forever. "Getting luckier every day," he said, the conviction in his words striking her with a force that stunned her.

"Look!" Becca yelled, racing through the screened door ahead of her brothers. She was wearing a bright orange sweatshirt that hung past her knees and sported the Texas Longhorns' logo, but it was the smile on her face that brightened the room. "Brad brought me a birthcake present." She placed a large package, gaily wrapped with wide ribbons and bows, on the table. "But I can't open it until tomorrow," she informed them solemnly.

Brad stood behind her in the doorway, his gaze connecting with Jake's. "It is okay?"

Jake looked a little uncomfortable. "Of course, it's okay, son. I plan to do some shopping of my own tomorrow."

Kendall felt a moment of trepidation, but this was something they had to work through by themselves. She had already bought her own present and had helped Josh, Timmy, and Matt pick out their gifts. Wrapped and hidden in her linen closet, they were ready for the festivities tomorrow afternoon. And from the looks of things, it was going to be a birthday to remember.

EIGHT

What the hell had made him think he could get through the day without Becky's memory cutting him to pieces? Jake shoved the beautifully wrapped package across the front seat and slid behind the steering wheel. Since noon, he'd walked up and down every aisle in every toy department in every store in Rosemont until he found just the right baby doll for Becca. He'd even remembered to pick out an appropriate birthday card. Over and over throughout the day, he'd had to force thoughts of Becky out of his mind, thoughts that ricocheted between his dead wife and Kendall Jamison. Now that he'd completed his shopping, there was nothing left to distract him.

He glanced at his watch. He'd left the house early this morning while everyone except Kendall and Brad were still sleeping. They were getting along like old friends, and maybe that rankled Jake more than he wanted to admit. Hell, everyone thought she was great, but why wouldn't they? She *was* great. She was well organized, she showed a genuine interest in each child as an individual, and her cooking was improving daily. She was bright and witty and caring—and too damned desirable for her own good. No, make that *his* own good.

Yeah, he conceded grudgingly, she was desirable, but it was more than a physical attraction that was eating at him. If that was all there was to it, he could handle it. But she made him *feel*. Good and happy and . . . alive.

That hit him where it hurt. Alive. He was alive. His kids were alive. Kendall was alive. The only things that had been dead until Kendall showed up were his emotions. Now they, too, were painfully alive and well, forcing him to feel again.

He shook the thoughts away with a vengeance. He wasn't ready for that kind of soul searching, especially today.

The party wouldn't start for another couple of hours, but he didn't want to go home and inflict his gloomy mood on his family. Jared and Leza would be there by now, helping out, so he wasn't really needed. Hell, who was he kidding? Today of all days, he wasn't in any mood to be around anyone, especially his family. Especially Kendall.

He gripped the steering wheel and squeezed his eyes shut. When he opened them, the first thing he saw was Willie Britt's Country Club. As he saw it, he had three choices: He could go home or visit the cemetery or—

He got out of his car and locked the door. Shooting the bull with Willie Britt and the boys was as good a way as any to kill a little time. And maybe some of his pain . . .

Everyone was having a good time, but Kendall was fuming. Where was Jake? She'd called the office at five and was told that no one had heard from him since lunch.

The party was supposed to start at four and everyone was anxious to get on with it, especially Brad and Josh. They'd promised to take Timmy and Matt camping after the party; they had to leave soon if they wanted to get to Cold Creek in time to pitch camp before nightfall.

She'd done everything humanly possible to make this day easier for Jake, and now he was pulling a disappearing act. Well, he could damn well make his own excuses when he decided to show up. She had a party to get back to. The kids had swum until their fingers and toes were pruney, and they were getting bored with the games. It was long past time to eat, and they still had to open presents and have cake and ice cream.

"Leza," she called from the back porch. "It'll be dark soon. We'd better not wait any longer."

Leza and Jared exchanged concerned looks. "I think you're right," they said at the same time and laughed. In the month she'd known them, she'd come to the conclusion that they were a perfect couple, a perfect family. That they loved and respected each other was as evident—

She chopped off the thought when she realized how close it came to being the very same one she'd had that first day in Jake's office as she studied the family portrait on his desk. Suddenly it struck her that something might have happened to him. If ever she'd known a family man, it was Jake Sentell. Barring anything catastrophic, nothing would keep him from spending the afternoon with his children on so special a day.

"He's all right," Leza said, catching her off guard. "If anything had happened, someone would have called."

Kendall felt a little foolish for being caught worrying

about a man like a . . . woman in love. Somehow the thought didn't surprise or alarm her. She should have admitted it sooner; now that she had, she realized she'd started falling in love with Jacob Sentell the moment he walked into his office and looked at her with those clear gray eyes.

She had been so sure she'd found love with Ellis. Looking back, she found it so easy to see how he had slowly, methodically pried each private and intimate detail about her past from her and had then used that information to zero in on her insecurities. Her father's desertion and her unhappy childhood became weapons in his seduction of her. But what hurt most was knowing that he'd uncovered and used her sense of protectiveness and guilt where Courtney was concerned. Few people knew about her deathbed promise to her mother to take care of Courtney. Even fewer knew the guilt she'd suffered from not being able to keep that promise. Was she ready to expose herself to that kind of intimacy with another man?

She didn't realize she hadn't responded to Leza's comment until Leza reached for the tray she was carrying.

"You're right, I know," she finally said, pushing the uneasy thoughts from her mind. "But where could he be?"

Leza set the tray on the table and leaned backward to stretch the kinks out of her back. "Knowing Jake, there's no telling. Someone probably needed help with something, and he lost track of time. It's an occupational hazard."

Kendall pulled a chair away from the table. "Would you sit down and stop doing so much? Look at your ankles. They're twice their normal size."

"Normal size?" Leza gave her a grin meant to procreate sympathy. "What's that?"

Although Kendall had never been pregnant, she definitely could sympathize. "When are you due?" She couldn't believe she hadn't asked before now.

"In two weeks," Leza answered with a weary sigh. "Actually, it's sixteen days and counting."

"Come and get it," Jared interrupted, holding up a platter of hamburger patties and hot dogs he'd been keeping warm. In Jake's absence, he'd stepped in to do the grilling. Seven hungry Sentell offspring began clamoring around the patio table, leaving little time for worry.

An hour later, just as Kendall slipped away to call the office one more time, she heard a car stopping in the circular drive out front. Wiping her hands on a cup towel, she stepped into the entry hall. She was surprised to see the deputy who'd shown her into Jake's office just over a month ago helping Jake out of his patrol car.

Stunned, she watched Jake stumble, laugh, and throw his arm around the deputy's shoulder. How they managed the front steps without inflicting bodily harm on each other was beyond her. Hurriedly she opened the screen door, giving Jake an angry "Shhh!"

"Hi ya, Jamison," he greeted her, oblivious to her shushing. His words slurred together; his eyes were glazed orbs of nickel gray. At her glower of disapproval, he tried to stand straight and sober. All he managed to do was lose his balance. The deputy saved him from winding up back outside on the porch by grabbing a handful of shirt.

"I'm okay, Bill." Again Jake tried to stand alone, again without success.

Drunk! Although her heart ached for him and his

pain, she couldn't believe he'd come home in this condition. Today of all days. She glanced over her shoulder. Fortunately no one else had heard the car.

"I can make it from here," he said to Bill, but his unsteady legs forced him to make a grab for Kendall.

Reflexively she grabbed back, lending the support he needed on the opposite side of Bill. "I don't think you can make it anywhere," she muttered through tight lips. Then to Bill she said, "Could you help me get him upstairs?"

"Be happy to." The deputy's expression was filled with understanding.

Making it up the stairs and down the hall to his room wasn't easy. Finally, Kendall and Bill stood over Jake's prostrate form sprawled across his bed.

"Sorry to bring him home like this," Bill said with a shake of his head. "But when Willie Britt called, I just wanted to get him home before anyone else saw how bad off he was." He straightened his shirt and gun belt, then ran his fingers through his curly auburn hair. "Haven't seen him like this in a long time." Then, as if he realized he'd said too much, he asked, "Can you handle him by yourself?"

Kendall didn't want to handle him. She wanted to strangle him. "I'm not alone," she said, leading him out of the room. "His brother and oldest son are here. Thank you for your help . . . Bill, isn't it?"

He nodded and followed her down the stairs. "Tell him I'll see him in church tomorrow—" He stopped and gave her an embarrassed smile.

Kendall felt positively wicked for the sense of satisfaction she felt knowing how bad Jake would probably feel in the morning. "I'll see to it personally that he's there on time." Having to get up early and face a congregation of friends and neighbors would serve him right.

She watched Bill get into his car and drive away before turning back to the kitchen. The back door opened and Jared appeared, silly chef's hat, barbecue-stained apron, leftovers and all.

"Was that Bill Woodyard I saw leaving?" he asked.

Kendall nodded and tucked a few strands of hair behind her ear that had fallen loose during her struggle with Jake. "He brought Jake home."

Jared didn't miss her disheveled state. "I was afraid of that," he said, glancing out into the backyard. "Pretty bad off, I take it."

"You could say that. He should sleep a while."

"It's a good thing the boys will be gone tonight. And I don't think Becca should see him . . . well, like he is. Why don't you let her go home with us?"

Leza would never complain, but Kendall knew she was exhausted. "Leza's pretty tired. I don't know . . ."

"Look, Kendall, I know we didn't get off to a very good start, but I want to help. He'll probably sleep it off and be no trouble at all. But just in case, I'd feel better if Becca went home with us. Between Maggie and me, we'll make sure she doesn't overdo."

His suggestion made more sense than taking a chance on Becca's seeing her father in a drunken stupor. Kendall gave Jared a smile of thanks. "I'll pack her things," she said.

By the time she returned with Becca's bag, Jared, Leza, and the older boys had cleared away the party debris and were waiting for her. Brad and Josh had their camping gear stowed in the cargo bed of Brad's pickup, and Jared and Leza were rounding up their boys and Becca.

"He'll be okay," Leza whispered and gave Kendall a hug. "See you at church in the morning?"

Kendall returned the gesture of friendship. "You bet." She went down on one knee to give Becca a kiss. "Happy birthday, sweetie. I'll see you tomorrow."

Becca threw her arms around her. "Thank you for my birthcake party. Did you save Daddy a piece of cake?"

As far as Kendall was concerned, he didn't deserve one. "Sure did. I'll give it to him . . . after he has his dinner," she promised.

A few minutes later, she'd helped Jared strap four toddlers into car seats and was waving good-bye from the steps of the back porch. Now, she told herself, a few last-minute details in the kitchen, then she could hit the shower and shampoo her hair, slip into her new robe, and curl up with one of her favorite authors for a few hours of uninterrupted reading before bedtime. Anything to keep from thinking about the stunt Jake had pulled—or that they were alone in the house for the night.

She'd just added the detergent to the dishwasher when the telephone rang. Half expecting it to be Jared or Leza calling to check on Jake, she answered on the second ring.

"Hey, girl, how's it going?" Nancy Bigelow sounded as though she was just next door instead of over two hundred miles away. They'd kept in touch since her move to Rosemont, and a phone call wasn't unusual. Still, Kendall couldn't ignore the sinking sensation that began to swirl and churn in the pit of her stomach.

"Better than I expected," she answered honestly. She knew she'd done well to overcome the awkward situation of taking the beloved Esther's place, facing Timmy's open hostility and Josh's crush on her, not to mention her own attraction to her employer. She was still somewhat shaken by her admission for her feelings for Jake, but all in all things were going well. Too well, perhaps . . .

"Glad to hear it."

The pause that followed reinforced Kendall's premonition of impending doom. "What's up, Nancy? You wouldn't have called, especially on a Saturday and at your own expense, unless there was a problem." Nancy always called from her office to save herself the price of a phone call.

Nancy's laugh sounded forced. "Good old straight-talking Kendall." Another pause. "Your Aunt Maxine called me a little while ago." For the first time, Kendall regretted ever having confided in Nancy. She'd been expecting something like this, but now that it had happened she wasn't ready to face it.

"*Courtney's* Aunt Maxine," she corrected, remembering the one and only time she'd met Maxine and Marilyn Blankenship. Shortly after her mother's death, the two spinster sisters had arrived from Dallas to take charge of Courtney. Kendall, seventeen at the time, had no legal recourse other than to let them take eleven-year-old Courtney. The memories were as clear and painful as they'd been that day, resurrecting the feelings of desertion and guilt she'd experienced watching Courtney go, crying and begging to stay with Kendall. Desertion because once again she was alone—this time truly alone. Guilt because she'd made her dying mother a promise that she would take care of Courtney, and she hadn't kept that promise.

"Yes, Courtney's aunt," she heard Nancy saying. "She wanted to know where you were. Said something about Courtney being in trouble again. Of course, I wouldn't give her your address and phone number, but I did promise to give you the message."

Trouble? Kendall had to fight back the urge to ask for details. Trouble was Courtney's middle name. By the time the Blankenship sisters had taken custody of Courtney, she had already been in trouble with school officials and the law. And after what Courtney and Ellis had done to her, why should Kendall care? Other than a few postcards, Courtney hadn't bothered to keep in touch, and that hurt Kendall almost as much as what had happened in Houston. Although she'd protected Courtney all these years, she'd vowed when she was released from Gatesville never to let her sister get that close to her again. Kendall's heart felt heavy, full of sorrow. Whether it was because of the deathbed promise she'd made to her mother or her love for Courtney, she did care.

She picked up the pen next to the notepad. "Did you get her number?" She jotted down the number Nancy gave her, chatted briefly about things friends discussed before they said their good-byes, then hung up and stared at the phone. She didn't want to make the call. She didn't want to know what Courtney was into now. She didn't want to care, and she certainly didn't want to get caught up in Courtney's life again. But she had to make sure her sister was okay.

The phone rang five, six, seven times, and Kendall was about to hang up when someone lifted the receiver.

"Miss Blankenship, this is Kendall Jamison." She had to force her voice to be casual. "Nancy Bigelow gave me your message."

"Oh, Kendall, dear, I'm so glad you called. I just don't know what to do about Courtney." Maxine Blankenship's concern manifested itself in the form of a jumble of run-on sentences.

"Slow down, Miss Blankenship. I can't understand you."

"I'm sorry, dear." Kendall heard in the older woman's voice that she was trying to school her thoughts. "Courtney came home several weeks ago, and Marilyn and I are worried sick."

"Is she okay?" was all Kendall really wanted to know.

"Why, yes. Physically she's fine. It's just that when we agreed to let her stay with us, she swore she was through with Ellis. But now she's started coming home late, when she bothers to come home at all, and then she slips out before Marilyn and I get up. I just know she's seeing that man—"

"Miss Blankenship," Kendall interrupted, not wanting to know any more, "I can appreciate how you feel, but quite honestly, I can't imagine why you'd think I'd want to get involved. I don't need the trouble Courtney can bring down on me. I'm sorry to be so blunt, but Courtney's almost twenty-three years old; it's time she—"

This time Maxine Blankenship cut Kendall off with a frantic, "But you're her sister. She'll listen to you."

"Just like she listened to me in Houston?" Kendall couldn't hide her sarcasm. "No, Miss Blankenship," she said, softening her tone for the older woman's benefit. "And being her *stepsister* hasn't meant anything in a long, long while, especially to her. I have to go now." She hung up before the woman could say anything more. And she felt rotten. She didn't doubt for a second that Courtney was in trouble again. But she couldn't, *wouldn't*, get involved. Not only would it jeopardize all she'd accomplished since her release from Gatesville, but it might compromise Jake in some way. Besides, she believed what she'd just told Miss Blankenship; it was time Courtney began to face the consequences for her actions.

A loud crash from upstairs startled her, forcing her thoughts away from the unpleasant topic of Courtney. An image of that wonderful old bedside lamp in Jake's room flashed through her mind.

Seconds later she stood before Jake's still-closed door, listening. From inside she heard his muttered, yet clearly discernible and colorful oaths. She opened the door, and, to her regret but not her surprise, she saw the shattered lamp on the floor at Jake's feet. Jake simply stood there staring down at the mess he'd made. Suddenly Kendall was transported to another room, another time. How many times had she helped her mother subdue a drunken Randall Blankenship?

Anger flooded her. Until he looked up and she saw the pain in his face. The lamp hadn't been the only fatality. Blood dripped from his left hand to sink into the plush pile of the deep jade carpet.

"Oh, Jake," she said, only vaguely realizing she'd called him by name. Her anger disappeared the instant she realized he was hurt. Suddenly she was beside him, leading him to the edge of the bed, where she made him sit down. She took his injured hand in her own. Close inspection showed that it looked worse than it was. Still, it needed tending. "Stay put," she told him, taking the time to stow all the broken pieces in the wastebasket. She remembered seeing a first-aid kit in the guest bathroom.

She returned to find Jake exactly where she'd left him. His injured hand rested on his left knee, soaking the denim with blood. She'd deal with that, as well as the carpet, later. Taking a clean towel she'd thought to grab on her way out of the bathroom, she knelt before

him and placed it under his hand before pouring perox-
ide over the open wound.

Jake tensed, his only reaction since she'd found him,
but he held still under her ministering hands. In a matter
of minutes, the cut in his palm was cleansed and band-
aged. She didn't think it needed stitches.

Kendall leaned back on her haunches. "There," she
said, raising her gaze. Along his jaw—that strong, an-
gular jaw that always tempted her to touch him—she
saw a streak of blood. His right hand, she noticed, was
smeared with blood also. She came up on her knees
and leaned toward him, wedging her torso between his
legs. With a clean corner of the towel, she wiped the
blood from his face. His hand came up to cover hers,
and looking up, Kendall knew what all those romance
novels meant when they spoke of the heroine "drowning in his smoldering gaze." His eyes were smoldering,
and she was drowning.

"Jake . . ." She wanted him to let go of her; she
wanted him to hold her. She wanted him—period.

He smiled, a crooked little smile that drew to life
that one adorable dimple in his left cheek. "Jake?" he
asked. "What happened to the ever-proper-and-imper-
sonal 'Sheriff'?" He was teasing her, and his voice was
husky and more seductive that she'd ever heard it.

And it gave her the impetus she needed to break the
spell she'd fallen under. "You haven't acted much like
the sheriff today," she rebuked, slapping the towel into
his hand and coming to her feet. "Or a father."

He wanted to answer her last remark, she could tell,
but he wasn't thinking clearly enough to make a worth-
while comeback. He tried to stand and couldn't, and she
decided a quarrel would be much too one-sided to be fair.

"Morning's going to come around awfully early for
you," she said without bothering to hide her censure.

"You take off your shirt and I'll tackle the boots, then get you in bed."

"That's the best offer I've had all day," he said, his words still slurring slightly. He plopped down on the bed, then tried to offer her his left foot. In the end she had to lift it for him. Turning her back, she straddled his leg and gave the boot a firm tug that sent her stumbling forward. Second boot, same result. She turned around to find him fumbling with the buttons of his shirt.

Gently stilling his clumsy fingers, she told him, "Here, let me help." The buttons fell away with ease. Her fingers brushed his shoulder, and as the shirt slid off, the cuffs hung up around his wrists. She'd forgotten to unbutton them. Sitting there with his hands literally cuffed behind him, his bare chest so broad and muscular and so very tempting, Kendall felt her mouth go dry, heard her breath catch in her throat. The heat from him radiated across the space separating them. Never had she wanted to touch a man so badly. From where she knelt she had a clear view of his jawline and throat. The pulse beating beneath his Adam's apple throbbed in time with her own. Hard, fast, rhythmic. What would he taste like?

Realizing the dangerous path her thoughts were taking, she reached behind him to release his hands. He didn't have time to try to stop her when she placed her hands on his knees to push herself up and away from him. The palm of her right hand felt warm and sticky. Glancing down, she remembered that his hand had bled all over him. She couldn't let him crawl into bed wearing blood-soaked jeans. He had to get out of them, or else he'd ruin the bedding. He was in no condition to object when she reached for his waistband and gave him a gentle push backward.

"Aw, Jamison," he drawled, "your timin' is awful. I don't think I'm in any shape to do you any good."

His remark was the closest thing to crude she'd ever heard him say, but before she could react, he wound his hand around the back of her neck and pulled her down on top of him.

"But I'll give it my best shot." He held her firmly while raising his head to claim her lips with a kiss that started out lazy and seductive. She caught the sigh of pleasure that threatened to escape from her when he gently took her bottom lip between his own lips. Then the kiss became more urgent, more intimate.

Lost in the moment, Kendall tasted the bourbon on his tongue, felt the hard evidence of his desire pressing against her pelvis. He was in better shape than he gave himself credit for, she thought dizzily.

"God, how I need you," he said, his breathy whisper against her throat igniting a longing inside her she had refused to acknowledge existed.

Somehow he managed to tug her blouse from the waistband of her jeans. His hand felt rough against her skin, his fingers sure and knowing in their quest for her breast. Then his lips found hers again.

"Kiss me back, Jamison," he whispered, his tongue lightly tracing her lips.

Jamison. Her last name spoken so casually in the heat of the moment was like being doused with ice water. She hid her hurt and anger by doing as he asked. She kissed him. Not the passionate kiss he expected. Not a peck to mollify him. Just a kiss. Still, the touch of his lips was so consuming that it filled her with a longing that made her ache because she couldn't, *wouldn't*, let herself have more. She broke the contact with a false smile and a forced giggle.

"Why don't *we* wash some of this blood off you?"

she said, intoning just the right degree of seductiveness to pique his interest. Letting her hands trail provocatively down the length of him as she stood, she waited for him to come to his feet.

It took very little coaxing to get him to the bathroom. Laughing and reaching for her while she turned on the cold water, he gave a surprised yelp when she shoved him into the shower and closed the door.

''That should cool you off, hot shot,'' she called, feeling triumphant and angry and more than a little regretful.

Downstairs, Kendall stepped out of the steaming shower, slipped on her robe, and quickly towel-dried her freshly shampooed hair. Maybe she should have used cold water, too. Jake's kisses had shaken her more than she wanted to admit. And his touch . . . even now she trembled at the memory of his warm, rough hand gently cupping, then kneading her breast. . . .

With an expletive she'd heard many times at Gatesville, she trudged off to her adjoining bedroom. She was angry with herself. She was angry with Jake. She was confused. Until he'd called her Jamison, she knew she'd have probably submitted to him. Which was silly. After all, it wasn't as though he'd called out another woman's name. In her heart she knew they would have been submitting to each other. Neither would have been the victor; neither would have been the loser. But how could she be sure she wouldn't have been just a substitution for his dead wife?

She grabbed her comb and dragged it through the length of her damp hair. The house was quiet. He must have gone back to bed. This time, still angry with herself, she grabbed her novel and curled up in the window seat to read.

NINE

Jake threw the sheet back and tried to stop his head from spinning. He felt like crap. But he didn't feel any sympathy for himself. He'd asked for it. Didn't he know better than anyone that drowning your sorrows never really helped? Especially when there were others to consider. The hangover he'd have in the morning would be rough, but the hard part would be later when he had to look into Becca's trusting eyes and tell her that he was sorry for missing her birthday party, the first party she'd ever had.

Then there was Jamison. . . .

He'd brushed his teeth and shaved after the cold shower he'd taken alone, but he could still taste and smell and feel her. He groaned aloud and shook his head in an attempt to rid himself of the memory. It was no use, and he knew he owed her an apology, not so much for wanting to make love to her, but for pawing her while he was sloppy drunk. Thank God he was sober enough to be embarrassed about that, but he'd have to really think about it later. Maybe food would make him feel better, at least physically.

He glanced at the clock on the bedside table. Eleven-thirty. Everyone should be in bed by now. With more effort than it normally took, he pulled on a clean pair of jeans and buttoned all but the top two buttons. Without bothering with his boots or shirt, he quietly made his way down the stairs. He'd raid the refrigerator and pray that food would help clear his head and dim this damned headache.

The house was still, but he saw a light under Kendall's door. She was still awake. Should he knock and get the apology out of the way or—

The decision was taken out of his hands when the door opened, leaving Kendall a shapely silhouette that made it hard for him to think clearly. Wearing her soft blue robe, her hair unbound and loose about her shoulders, she was more beautiful and desirable than he'd ever seen her. How the hell was he supposed to apologize for kissing her, for touching her, when all he wanted was to work the knot out of her belt, slip the robe from her . . . ?

Almost as though she could read his thoughts, she pulled the lapels of her robe closer together, then tightened the sash around her trim waist. Her gaze quickly took in his half-dressed state before she stepped on into the kitchen, flipped the light switch, and placed her book on the bar.

"You must be hungry," she said, opening the fridge and taking out the makings for sandwiches. "How many sandwiches do you want?"

"Two'll be fine," he answered, amazed that she was even speaking to him after the fiasco in his bedroom. "About earlier," he began, wanting to get it over. "I won't insult you with excuses—"

"Sheriff," she broke in, "the only person you owe

an apology is Becca. She was very disappointed that you weren't here today."

Jake wasn't sure why she was letting him off the hook, but he knew she was right about Becca. "Yeah, I know." He rubbed the back of his neck. "Where is she, by the way? She wasn't in her room. Did she talk the boys into taking her with them?"

"Of course not," Kendall answered, her laugh sounding forced. "Even if she had, I wouldn't have let her go. The boys needed some time alone with Brad. Jared and Leza took her home with them. Your brother didn't think it would be good for her to see you . . . well, let's just say in your condition."

He heard the censure in her tone, and maybe because he already felt guilty about his behavior, it angered him. He wasn't a boy who needed to be patronized. "Why don't you just call it like it was, Jamison? Drunk. I was sloppy, staggering, falling-down drunk."

"Okay," she said stiffly, her features changing from soft and beautiful to rigid and condemning. "If that's the way you want it. We didn't want her seeing you drunk. We didn't want her to know that instead of coming home on her birthday you decided to hang out at Willie Britt's and drink yourself senseless. I don't know what's wrong with you—"

"And it's none of your business," he shot back, turning and heading for the door. What had started off cordial enough had suddenly turned nasty. To make matters worse, his head hurt like hell.

"Sheriff."

He stopped without turning around.

"Things have been tense between us for weeks now. Have I done something that bothers you?"

There it was. Laid out in the open. He faced her.

"Everything you do bothers me." Simple and to the point.

"Is it because I've made changes in the routine?"

"Of course not. Things needed changing."

That seemed to spur her bravado. "You're right about that," she said. "Esther spoiled your children like an obsessive grandmother, and I can't believe how she encouraged you to wallow in the past the way she did. If I had to bet, I'd say that nothing, not one single thing in this house, has been changed since your wife died." She was on a roll now, and he knew he couldn't stop what was coming.

"You own the same car and the same furniture. The boys' rooms are outdated; their wallpaper and bedspreads and drapes are far too immature for them. And Becca's still sleeping in her crib, for goodness sake. She should have been in a regular bed at least six months ago." She stopped to catch her breath, and the way she looked at him made him feel lower than gum stuck to a shoe sole. "And how could you *never* have had a party for her?"

"That's enough, Jamison." He'd listened to all he cared to. "You don't know what you're dealing with here."

"Well, tell me, damn it!"

He usually controlled his anger. It was one of the things that separated him from the criminals he went after. Even so, he felt the old rage building inside him, rage at the unfairness of life—and at himself for not having been more careful about Becky. Now Kendall had pushed him over the edge.

"Becky died giving birth to Becca." He spit out the words as if they were something vile. "Today will always be the day she died. How can I celebrate that?"

Her eyes glinted like blue topaz. "That doesn't wash,

Sheriff. I'm not blind, and I'm certainly not stupid. I've known for some time that today's the anniversary of Becky's death. I understand how hard all this has been on you, but there's more to it than that. Maybe it would help to talk about—''

"Don't push this, Jamison." His voice broke with emotion. She was getting close to the truth, too damned close. God, he needed another couple of aspirin. He turned on his heels.

She caught up with him at the bottom landing of the staircase and stopped him by grabbing his arm. "I'm not an old drinking buddy or some guy you work with. My name's Kendall, Sheriff. Why won't you use it?"

Why wouldn't she just leave him alone? He'd never been able to face the fact that he'd contributed to Becky's death instead of protecting her as he'd promised. How could he explain it to Kendall? He was thankful she'd given him an out by calling him on his habit of referring to her as Jamison.

"Because calling you Kendall makes you more than my housekeeper." Even to him his words sounded as if it hurt to say them. "I can't afford to think of you any other way."

"Because you're afraid—"

He hadn't planned to reach out and grab her. He didn't mean to kiss her so hard that it forced a startled gasp from her. There was no gentleness in him, only raw, unbridled passion. He'd held himself in check for so long, and now that he'd touched her, he wasn't sure he could stop.

Her hands came up in protest, an impotent struggle that ended the moment he whispered her name.

"Kendall," he said against her lips, his voice an unrecognizable rasp even to him. "Beautiful Kendall," he said again, feeling a mixture of relief and exhilaration when her arms slipped around his neck, pulled him closer.

She was kissing him now. Hungry, urgent kisses that were fuel to the flames already burning out of control. The wall was at her back, her head pressed against it, giving his mouth access to the slender column of her neck, the tender contour of her throat.

He had to touch her, wanted to give her pleasure while he still could. He felt for the belted front of her robe, made quick work of the knot. The robe fell open, baring her to his gaze, his touch. She wasn't wearing a stitch underneath. Perfection. Tall and voluptuous and more beautiful than he'd ever imagined, she tested his restraint as a considerate lover to the limit.

Somewhere in the deepest recesses of his mind he knew he should be more gentle, take more time. But she wasn't making it easy.

"Jake," she whispered against his mouth.

His name on her lips broke his control. He felt her legs give way beneath her, and together they sank to the stairs. His fingers tangled in her hair, that glorious mane of red-gold that had haunted his dreams. Everything about her was soft, supple, drugging. He couldn't get enough. Their lips fused, nipped, teased, taunted.

He dragged his mouth from hers. "Tell me to stop." He kissed her again. Urgently. Hungrily. "Tell me you don't want this." He couldn't get enough of her.

"No." She tugged at the buttons on his jeans, and for him there was no turning back.

Their coming together was anything but tender. It was white-hot heat, total possession by each of the other. Never had Jake been so consumed by his need for a woman.

She cried out his name against his shoulder, and he felt the tremors of her release surround him. Only then did he allow himself his own pleasure, pleasure that was so consuming that he was blinded by the wonder of their union.

Lying still beneath him, her head resting on one of the steps, she raised her hand to caress his cheek. All it took was her touch to stir his passion again. He shifted his weight off her, and what he saw in her eyes tore at his soul. She cared for him. How could he be sure that he hadn't taken his guilt and his anger out on her, trying to rid himself of his pain?

"My God, what have I done?" He didn't realize he'd said the words aloud until the light of love shining in her eyes dimmed, then faded completely.

Firmly she pushed him away. Then she reached for her robe and slipped it on. "Nothing of any real consequence, Sheriff."

She left him then, alone on the stairs, and the sound of her sobbing behind her closed door knifed through him. He sat there a long while listening, knowing that she would send him away if he went to her now, wouldn't believe him if he told her what was in his heart. He didn't believe it himself. He'd always considered himself lucky that he'd found love so young in life. Never had he expected to be lucky enough to find it again.

He stepped into his jeans, but instead of going upstairs, he entered his study. Tonight no cozy fire warmly invited him in. Moonlight filtered through the gauzy panels covering the French doors, fell across the family portrait hanging above the mantelpiece. He crossed the darkened room to stand beneath it, and the memory of the day he and Becky hung it there tugged gently at his heart. Then his eyes came to rest on Becky's face. Only tonight the smile he'd always remembered as filled with happiness was different. Serene. Content. At peace.

And, oddly, for the first time in years, Jake felt all of those things.

He slipped off his wedding band, held it between his thumb and forefinger for a moment before he laid it on his desk. Then he raised his head and smiled back at his Becky.

Carefully reaching up, he took the portrait down and carried it upstairs to the master bedroom. He stood there in the room he'd come to hate and felt a tidal wave of relief wash over him. At last, he was free of the past.

Kendall had done that for him.

Kendall slept fitfully, waking before her alarm went off. After dressing for church, she made her way to the kitchen. Her night of crying and berating herself for not stopping Jake when she could have left her feeling sick and weak inside. The thought of food made her stomach churn, but the boys would be home soon, and Jake was sure to be starving. The lunch meat and mayo still lay on the breakfast bar where she'd left them before—

She couldn't think about it. Not now. Not ever. It hadn't happened the way she'd dreamed it would. *My God, what have I done?* His words shrilled through her brain again, as they had over and over throughout the long and torturous night. Obviously he regretted that it had happened at all. How could she live with that . . . ?

She knew Jake was in the room before he spoke, before she turned to see him standing in the doorway. He too was dressed for Sunday services. The navy suit and crisp white shirt were a stark contrast to his dark and virile good looks, but a closer look revealed features that were pale and drawn.

"Are you all right?" He sounded as tired as he looked.

Kendall didn't want to talk, didn't trust herself to speak without her feelings boiling out to embarrass her. "I should be asking you that," she countered. "I have some Alka Seltzer, if you—"

"Stop it, Kendall." He spoke softly, but he was more serious than she'd ever seen him. "Pretending it didn't happen won't make it so."

"I know."

"I didn't mean . . . did I hurt you?"

"No, I'm fine." The concern she saw on his face was sincere. "Honest."

He moved into the center of the room, still several feet from her. "I would have understood if you hadn't been here this morning."

"Why wouldn't I be here?"

"Because of what I did . . ."

"What you did?" She felt like a parrot repeating him.

He ran his fingers through his dark hair. "You didn't have that coming." He rubbed the back of his neck so hard that Kendall winced. "I'm the law in these parts, and what I did came very close to rape. It was inexcusable."

She didn't know what to say to that. Granted, he had been rough, but he hadn't forced her to do anything she hadn't wanted to do.

"So why are you still here?"

"Honestly," she answered, training her eyes on him; "because, like I said, you didn't hurt me. And you would have stopped if I'd told you to." She knew it, even if he didn't.

Her words seemed to relieve some of the guilt she saw in his eyes. "Is that all?" he asked after a moment of silence.

She didn't hesitate a second. "And I wanted it, too." *I want you to love me the way I love you.* She felt the heat of his gaze on her face and longed for him to say something, anything, to make the strain between them go away.

"So you're staying."

As long as you'll let me, she wanted to say, but all she could do was nod and stir the scrambled eggs.

"What's to keep it from happening again?"

She stopped stirring and met his gaze. "Me." She placed the spoon on the spoon rest. "Just because I didn't stop you doesn't mean I want it to happen again." She couldn't continue to look at him. "At least not like that." The eggs were sticking to the skillet, and she took them up. She spooned his portion onto a plate with two strips of bacon and two pieces of toast, then placed the plate on the bar.

Jake sat down and absently rearranged his breakfast with his fork while she poured them each a cup of coffee. Finally, without having taken a single bite, he put his fork down. "It's a little late to be asking this, but . . ."

Kendall felt the color drain from her face. She hadn't thought about it before, but she knew before she heard the words what he wanted to know.

". . . are you protected?"

"Well . . . no . . ." she stammered, trying to form a coherent thought. "But it's the wrong time of the month . . . I mean, it's the right time—" Did she *know* what she meant?

"It's okay, Kendall. I understand. But that doesn't mean you can't be pregnant." He shoved his plate away, then stood. "If you are, I won't shirk my responsibility. I'll be here for you."

His expression was solemn, and his words were still

echoing inside her head when he took his keys from the peg by the back door. "I have a few things to take care of in the barn. I'll bring the car around front in a while and be waiting for you and the boys," he said. "I'm going to ask Leza if she feels up to helping you redo the house. That is, if you want to tackle the job. You can start with Becca's room." Another surprise that left her speechless. "By the way, what's your favorite color?"

"Blue," she managed to say, not knowing which surprised her more—his off-handed question or that he had called her Kendall instead of Jamison.

Things had changed. But how?

Jake's stomach felt queasy and the pain behind his eyes was intense. He wished he'd taken Kendall up on the Alka Seltzer. His five children sat between him and Kendall on the hard wooden pew, but he occasionally glimpsed her out of the corner of his eye. Becca sat next to her, holding the hymnbook upside down. He heard Kendall's voice over Brad's, which was deep, and Josh's, which changed from tenor to alto without warning or intent. This morning she had left her hair down but had pulled it back on each side with gold combs. He noticed a tiny whisker burn on the underside of her small, proud chin, and he had to force from his mind the image of her lying naked beneath him on the stairs. Church was not the place for such thoughts.

No matter what she told him, he knew he had hurt her. Not physically, although their lovemaking had been anything but tender, but his words afterward had cut through her. She had no way of knowing what had gone through his mind. She probably thought he regretted their making love. The expression on her face last night as he rose up off her had taken him completely off guard. And until he'd seen her love for him in her face, he hadn't realized how much he felt for her. And to think there was a chance that he might have gotten her pregnant—

It was a painful thought, but one that could not be ignored or denied. God help him if anything happened to her because of him. As it had to Becky . . . Everything he'd said to her since last night had been wrong. He damned himself for a fool. How could he have stood there so calmly this morning and told her he wouldn't shirk his responsibility? He wouldn't, of course, but not because he might have gotten her pregnant. Hell, if he wasn't so scared of something happening to her, he'd want nothing more than a baby, their baby, to bind them together forever.

Forever. He felt a warming in his soul that had been cold and dead for too long. Forever with Kendall wouldn't be nearly long enough.

Again he glanced down the pew at her. Her voice rang sweet and clear above the others that weren't so sweet and clear, and he felt a smile coming from the inside of him. Since Kendall had come into his life, things would never be the same. He didn't want them to be the same. Lord, how he prayed he hadn't hurt her so badly that he wouldn't be able to convince her how much he wanted her, now and forever. And if she was pregnant . . . well, he'd just have to trust in his Maker that she would be okay.

Kendall and the children were standing together away from the flow of worshipers filing out of the church when three women approached them—a young woman approximately Brad's age, one roughly Kendall's age, and an older woman who gave every appearance of having descended from royalty. Kendall had met many of Jake's friends and neighbors after morning worship over the weeks, but she had never seen these three before. In spite of the night she'd had, until the absurdly overdressed trio headed toward them, their eyes taking mental measure of Kendall, she had felt like sunshine on a spring day in her new sundress and jacket of white eyelet. Stubbornly, she refused to be intimidated and straightened to her full height of five-ten.

The youngest of the threesome spoke first. "Hi, Brad. I didn't know you were in from Austin."

"Vanna," Brad returned, although he wasn't as animated in his greeting.

The oldest woman eyed Kendall as though she were a dirty spot on her carpet. "Where are your manners, Brad Sentell?" she said, her frosty manner reinforcing Kendall's resolve to be prepared for an assault. "Aren't you going to introduce us?"

Brad inched closer to Kendall. "I'm sorry, Mrs. Tyler. This is our new housekeeper, Kendall Jamison. Kendall, this is Mrs. Tyler, her daughter-in-law, Mrs. Prescott-Tyler, and her granddaughter, Vanna."

Now three sets of eyes openly scrutinized her. "Nice to meet you," Kendall said to all three women.

"So this is the sheriff's new housekeeper," the elder Mrs. Tyler said to Mrs. Prescott-Tyler. They exchanged glances.

Kendall was sure she wasn't imagining that Josh stepped closer to her on the opposite side of his brother or that Timmy and Matthew gathered in front of her like a protective human barrier. Becca tugged at her hand, and she picked the child up and settled her on her left hip.

"I must apologize for not dropping by to welcome you to Rosemont, Miss Jamison, but we've been to

Europe on holiday." Mrs. Tyler tilted her head down to peer over her glasses. "It is *Miss* Jamison, isn't it?"

"Yes, it is, Mrs. Tyler."

Another exchange of glances.

"I knew Jake was looking for someone to replace Esther," Mrs. Tyler's daughter-in-law said, "but I thought he wanted someone, well, a woman a little more mature. I offered to help him find someone, but then we left the country. How did he find you?"

Kendall searched the crowd until she found Jake talking with his brother and Leza on the opposite side of the churchyard. "We have a mutual acquaintance who recommended me to him." Until one of them openly opened fire, she would play the polite game.

"Oh, I see." This time it was Mrs. Tyler doing the speculating. "I don't mean to be judgmental, Miss Jamison, but do you think it's proper for you to be living in the same house—"

"Mrs. Tyler," Brad cut her off and slipped his arm around Kendall's waist in a protective display of support. "Kendall's living arrangements in my father's home are no concern of yours, but I'll be glad to put your mind at ease. There are four other people living under the same roof, and my father would never do anything that wouldn't look right to his kids."

"Yeah," Timmy piped up. "And Kendall ain't like that, neither."

Mrs. Tyler's face blanched. Mrs. Prescott-Tyler's lips pinched. Vanna smiled and turned her face away.

Kendall stifled a giggle. "It's 'Kendall *isn't* like that, *either*,' " she corrected Timmy's grammar with an affectionate ruffle of his hair. "And thank you, Timmy. Mrs. Tyler, I'm sure you'll understand if I tell you that I don't think this is something we should discuss now. If you'd like to come by the house one day for tea, I'll answer any questions you might have about my work, if you're truly interested in the ins and outs of being a housekeeper and nanny." She leveled her gaze at her, then at Mrs. Prescott-Tyler. "My personal life is no one's business but my own."

"I see you've met the Tylers." Jake's voice startled everyone except the children, who obviously had seen him approaching. He stepped between Brad and Kendall, took Becca, then put his arm around Kendall's waist in the same protective manner his son had. "Did you have a good trip?"

Vanna was the only one capable of speaking. "Mr. Sentell, you should have seen Paris. And Venice. Have you ever been to Europe?"

Jake laughed at the girl's excitement. "Only once, and it was on business, so I didn't get out much. You'll have to fill me in on what to see and do, in case I ever get the chance to go back."

Neatly changing the subject, Jake then excused his family and left a flustered Mrs. Tyler and Mrs. Prescott-Tyler to find someone else to try to intimidate. "I should have told you earlier how great you look today," he said, and Kendall wasn't at all surprised that he'd zeroed in on her insecurity.

"Thanks," she answered, feeling color stain her cheeks. "And thank you for stepping in when you did. They're quite . . ."

"Full of themselves."

"That's not what they're full of," Brad said. "Vanna wouldn't be so bad if she weren't so easily influenced by those two vipers." He gave a great sigh. "Boy, I'm glad you had enough sense not to get involved with Marianne after Mom died."

There was an awkward silence that Kendall felt obligated to fill. "Marianne?"

"Mrs. Prescott-Tyler," Jake clued her in. "And you needn't have worried, son. Jared and I have known Marianne since high school and know better than to get anywhere near the widow Tyler."

So Marianne Prescott-Tyler was a widow. Before Kendall could find out more about the woman, Jake turned to her.

"I need to go by and pick up my patrol car. Then I'll treat you guys to Sunday dinner. How's that sound?"

"Great . . . oh, boy . . . yea!!" all said at once.

Jake felt better now that he'd eaten. He was glad, though, that everyone except Brad had wanted to ride home in the station wagon with Kendall. For the most part, his kids were well behaved, but seven people in one car were hard on a man with a hangover.

"Head still hurt?"

Jake shifted his attention from the road to Brad. "A little."

Brad chuckled. "Hangovers are a bitch, aren't they?" He looked surprised that he'd sworn in front of his father, but Jake let it slide.

"Just nature's way of reminding you who's the boss." Jake could tell that something other than his father's headache was on Brad's mind. "I'm all ears, son. You didn't want to ride with me for my sparkling wit."

"Never could put anything over on you, could I?"

"Well, there were the girlie books Kendall found under my mattress."

Brad turned a strange shade of red.

Jake laughed. "You'll be glad to know your brothers didn't rat on you. The issue dates gave it away. Even Josh was too young to buy them when you were in high school."

"What did you do with them?"

"They went up in smoke."

"Even Veronica Valentine's centerfold?"

"*Especially* Veronica Valentine's centerfold."

They exchanged smiles, then rode in silence for a few more minutes. Jake wasn't one to push his kids to share with him.

Finally, Brad spoke up. "Dad, this is the only time I'll have to talk with you alone. I'll be leaving as soon as we get home."

"Sounds serious. Is there a problem at school?"

"No, nothing like that. And I don't need any extra money. I manage on what I earn. It's Kendall."

Jake glanced over at his son again. "What about her?"

"I just wanted you to know that I like her."

"Good. So do I."

"You do?" Brad sounded a bit flustered.

"Sure. What's not to like?"

"My point exactly."

"What do you mean?"

"Just that it's good to have a woman in the house again."

Jake couldn't help laughing. "Esther would love hearing that."

"That's not what I meant. Esther's . . . well, she's Esther. Kendall's . . . different. Special. You know?"

"Yeah, I know."

"And, Dad . . ." Brad hesitated. "If Mom could tell you what to do, she'd say go for it. Kendall's got a lot to offer this family, and if you'd admit it, you have a lot to offer her. I don't think she's had too much happiness in her life. Till now."

"How'd you get so smart in just nineteen years?"

"I had a good teacher who was an even better example."

They rode in silence for another few minutes. Finally, Jake admitted, "I may have blown it with her."

"Because of yesterday?"

Jake knew Brad couldn't have known about last night. "Yeah, because of yesterday."

"I remember my first bad case of puppy love and how miserable I was. Cindy Trahan, remember?"

"I remember."

"You took me camping down by the creek and we talked. You told me to take things slow and easy, to show her how much I liked her, then when the time was right to tell her how I felt."

Jake felt a grin creep across his face. "How'll I know when the time is right?" It was the same question Brad had asked him that long-ago day.

Brad smiled and reached over and put his hand on Jake's shoulder, just as Jake had done ten years ago on the bank of Cold Creek. "I can't tell you that, Dad. You'll just know."

Jake chuckled. Simple advice though it was, it was still the right advice. This was one of those moments that made life good.

"I'm glad you came home, son. I'll miss you when you leave." And it was true. The bond Jake and his oldest son shared went beyond special.

"I know, Dad."

TEN

The portrait was gone. Kendall stopped dusting the bookshelves and did a double take to make sure she wasn't seeing things. Or rather that she wasn't *not* seeing things. It had been there Friday when she straightened Jake's study, so what had happened to it?

She took a step toward the fireplace, but the ringing of the telephone stopped her. "Sentell residence," she answered, listening while the man on the other end of the line asked for Jake. "I'm sorry, he's not here. Have you tried his office?"

"Yes, but they said he was on his way home. Would you have him call me when he gets there?"

Jake hadn't said anything this morning about coming home for lunch, and he hadn't called from the office later to tell her that his plans had changed. He liked spending extra time with Becca, but it wasn't like him to just pop in on them without notice. Still, things like this happened. She could whip up something tasty for him when he got here.

"Of course." She put down the dust cloth and

reached for the pen lying on the desk blotter. Something caught her eye. Next to the lamp she saw Jake's wedding band. She picked it up and held it in the palm of her hand. Nothing special, just a plain gold band, its shape warped slightly by years of wear, but she'd never seen him without it. Instinctively, she glanced over her shoulder at the bare spot above the mantelpiece.

"Are you there?" the caller asked loudly.

"Yes, I'm here. I couldn't find a piece of paper."

"It's okay. He has my number. Just tell him Dale Patterson called."

From outside she heard a car coming down the driveway. "I think I hear him now, Mr. Patterson. Do you mind holding while I hurry him up?"

"Not at all."

Kendall placed the receiver on Jake's desk; then, remembering to put the ring back where she'd found it, she hurried to the kitchen.

"There's a Mr. Patterson holding the line for you in your study," she told Jake when he stepped inside the door.

He discarded his Resistol on his way through the kitchen. "Is Becca down for her nap yet?"

"No, she's watching *Sesame Street* in the den."

"Good. I have a surprise for both of you," he called from down the hall.

A surprise? That would explain the unexpected daytime visit. But what was the explanation about the portrait and his wedding band? She was still pondering both when Jake returned a few minutes later with a giggling Becca in his arms.

"Nana and Poppa want you and the boys to come for a visit during spring break," he was telling her.

Becca clapped her tiny hands. "Oh, boy. Matt told

me Nana makes banana puddin' and Poppa takes ever'-
body fishin'.''

"That was my father-in-law," Jake explained to
Kendall. "They usually take the boys for a couple of
weeks during the summer. This year, they're planning
an extended vacation and want to see them before they
go. I figured it would be a good time for you and Leza
to get started on the house."

Kendall looked at Becca's smiling cherub face and
felt shaken. "But Becca's so little," she said, reaching
for the toddler. Just the thought of the child being so
far away left her heart feeling as empty as her arms.

Jake's features softened. "She's never gone before,
but Betty wants her to come this time." Kendall heard
in his voice that he was trying to console her. "Besides," he went on, "Fort Worth's no more than two
hours away. If it doesn't work out, we can just pick
up and go get her."

Kendall's first concern, of course, was for Becca,
but she would miss the child terribly. She would miss
them all, but the boys were gone so much, and she and
Becca were together almost every waking moment. She
hadn't realized how strong the bond between them had
grown until she was faced with the prospect of Becca's
not being with her. And then there was the fact that
with the children gone, she and Jake would be alone
for almost two weeks.

"Really, Kendall, it'll be okay." Every time he
called her Kendall, she remembered the first time he'd
said it—while making love to her on the stairs. Not
once since had he reverted to calling her Jamison.

"They aren't strangers," she heard him saying over
the roaring in her ears that the memory always evoked.
"They're her grandparents." He reached out and took

Kendall's hand. "Now, for that surprise." Leading her to the back door, he told her to close her eyes.

When he told her she could open them, she saw a dark blue and metallic silver Suburban parked beside the station wagon. The sticker was still in the window, and the vehicle was sporting dealer plates.

"Since I'm such a Dallas Cowboys fan, suppose I could get away with a big blue star on each front door?" he asked, feigning just a touch of uncertainty.

They both laughed, and Kendall found herself wanting to play along. "I don't see why not. And since you're the sheriff, you'd be killing two birds with two stars." This time they both grimaced at their silliness.

This was a side of Jake that she'd seen more and more often of late. That they could share something this absurd gave Kendall a warm and wondrous sense of belonging. She had to say or do something to keep her feelings from showing.

"It's a beautiful car . . . truck . . . ?" She laughed at not knowing what to call the vehicle.

Slowly Jake's expression sobered. "Someone made me realize that it's time I made some changes around here." He handed her the keys, giving her hand a gentle squeeze as he did. "I just came home to pick up the wagon. Got a hell of a trade-in for it." Before Kendall knew what had happened, he gave them each a quick peck on the check, grabbed his hat, and left.

She watched him go, knowing in her heart that the missing portrait and Jake's wedding band were just the beginning of good things yet to come.

School let out early for the holiday that following Friday. Kendall and Becca picked up the boys at noon, and they all struck out for Fort Worth in the Cowboy-Suburban like a pioneer family heading West. Jake had to be in court all day and asked if Kendall would mind the drive alone with the children. Interstate 20 West would take them all the way to Dallas, he told her. From there Josh knew how to get to the Pattersons' Lake Worth home. She suspected that Jake would have found another reason, any reason, to ask her to make the trip. She knew that he was sympathetic to her fears about Becca's first stay away from home.

Now, driving home alone, she had to admit that she felt much better after meeting the Pattersons and getting a look at where her children would be staying.

Her children? Her hands tightened on the steering wheel. When had she started thinking of Jake's children as her own? What a dangerous trap she could be setting for herself. After their talk Sunday morning, neither had mentioned their lovemaking again. Although she was aware of the subtle difference in Jake's attitude toward her, she hadn't dared to hope for anything more. His wedding band and the missing portrait were still mysteries, but other than their easy camaraderie and the peck on her cheek the morning he'd brought home the Suburban, he'd said or done nothing else to reinforce her optimism concerning their relationship. So, if she let herself think in terms of *her* children or her place in their lives, she could be setting herself up for one hell of a heartache. And she'd had enough of that to last a lifetime.

Shaken by her train of thought, she took the next exit and pulled into a parking space at an interstate restaurant. She'd left the Pattersons without accepting their invitation to stay for dinner, and now that she'd reached the outskirts of Dallas she was getting hungry. She'd take advantage of the time it took to grab a quick bite to regroup, then get on back to Rosemont.

Taking her keys and grabbing her purse, she stepped

down from the driver's side of the Suburban, but a flier taped to the inside of the glass door of the restaurant stopped her from going inside.

LITTLE MISS METROPLEX PAGEANT . . .

She scanned the rest of the information printed on the bulletin. Ellis hadn't changed the wording one iota in all these years.

With everything that had happened between Jake and herself, her conversation with Courtney's aunt had been the last thing on her mind. She remembered Miss Blankenship telling her that Courtney had been in Dallas for several weeks, plenty of time for her and Ellis to set up a new baby pageant scheme. Now that she thought about it, and knowing both Courtney and Ellis as she did, they had probably argued, sending Courtney running to her aunts. Which could prove disastrous for Ellis. Courtney knew enough about his scams to put him away for a lot of years, and she wasn't above turning on him if she felt threatened in any way. He couldn't afford to let Courtney out of his sight for long, and Kendall could imagine the win-back campaign he'd launched. Courtney was no match for him when he turned on the charm, especially if he wanted her back badly enough.

Torn between wanting to do what was right—call the authorities with what she knew about Ellis's scam—and her love for Courtney, Kendall stood there staring at the flier while she tried to bring her breathing back to normal. Regardless of what she had told Maxine Blankenship, she realized she couldn't do anything, including leave Dallas, until she knew for sure whether Courtney was still mixed up with Ellis.

She dug in her purse until she found a pen, jotted down the phone number, then scrounged around for a quarter for the pay phone she saw just inside the door.

With her heart hammering wildly inside her chest, she dialed. A sick feeling in the pit of her stomach replaced the hammering the instant she recognized Courtney's voice.

A couple of seconds ticked by before Kendall found her voice. "Corky?"

A pause fraught with tension followed. "Yes, this is the Little Miss Metroplex Pageant. How can I help you?"

"Ellis is there, right?"

"That's right. I'll be glad to send you the information you need. May I have your name and address?"

"Corky, I'm in Dallas . . . at the . . ." She looked around until she found the sign identifying the restaurant. ". . . Tejas Cafe on I-Twenty East. Do you know where that is?"

"Yes, I have it. It'll be in the mail before we close for the day."

Kendall glanced at her watch. "I'll wait for you until six, if you can make it. We need to talk, Cork."

Another pause. Courtney's voice sounded funny when she finally said, "You're welcome. Hope to see you soon."

The dial tone sounded in Kendall's ear and she blinked away the tears. Something was wrong. Courtney had sounded . . . what . . . ? Frightened? Kendall was afraid that she might be letting herself in for God only knew what, but, Lord, something was wrong.

She wasn't hungry anymore but took a booth toward the back of the dining room, where she nursed a glass of iced tea while she waited. Unable to stop her thoughts from racing around and over each other, she fingered her keys nervously. One minute she fretted about Courtney, the next she questioned her own good sense for even taking a chance on getting involved with her again. And, of course, there was that part of her that wanted to do the right thing and damn the consequences—turn them both in.

At last Courtney came through the door. Kendall laid her keys aside and waited for her sister to spot her; when she finally did, Kendall gave her a tentative smile. Courtney looked different, older, of course, but tired and ragged, not as self-confident. She sure as hell didn't look twenty-three years old. Or happy.

Kendall stood up, and Courtney hesitated just short of the table.

"You look great, Kenny. . . ."

Kendall heard the crack in her voice and all the ill will ebbed from her. She took the two steps necessary to gather Courtney in her arms, and they clung to each other the way they had on those terrible nights when Courtney's father had come home drunk and spoiling for a fight.

"So do you, Corky." It was one of the few times she allowed herself the luxury of a little white lie. "Are you hungry? I haven't ordered yet."

"Maxine and Marilyn will have supper waiting." Courtney sat down in the seat Kendall had vacated, scooting Kendall's handbag across the vinyl seat as she did. "Is that how you knew how to find me? Did they call you?"

Kendall sat opposite her. "My parole officer in Houston relayed a message from Maxine. I returned the call but told her I wouldn't help . . ." She held Courtney's gaze. "I was on my way home from Fort Worth when I stopped for something to eat. I saw the notice about the pageant in the window and couldn't leave without knowing for sure if you were involved with it or not." She paused when the waitress approached for their order.

"Just bring me a slice of sweet potato pie and a glass of milk," Courtney told her, looking at Kendall.

"Nothing for me." Kendall waited for the waitress to finish writing down Courtney's order. "Corky, why are you still doing this?" she asked after the woman left. There was a desperate edge to her voice. Lord, she was torn between being angry and being frightened for Courtney. "Wasn't what happened to me lesson enough for you? And I was innocent of any wrongdoing." She didn't think it possible for Courtney's face to lose more color; she was wrong.

"Kenny, I'm so sorry about all that."

Kendall knew they wouldn't be able to discuss her imprisonment without hard feelings coming into play. Right now, the only thing on her mind was making her sister see that Ellis was bad news. Maybe it was wishful thinking, but there might still be hope for Courtney.

"Forget it. I have," she lied again. Courtney seemed to bring out the liar in her. "I was sure that by now you'd have gotten wise to Ellis. Corky, it's a downhill proposition with him, haven't you learned that by now?"

"I know." Even though Courtney agreed, she sounded defeated.

The waitress showed up with the pie and milk. Courtney picked up her fork and poked at the crust, giving Kendall a moment to think.

"Corky, you have to get away from him. It's not just you anymore. You have a child to think about." Maybe a guilt trip would work.

Courtney looked as though she'd been slapped in the face. "How did you know that?"

If Kendall heard the note of fear in Courtney's voice, she was too upset to notice it. "You told me, remember? I found your note after you and Ellis skipped out on me. The only reason I didn't drag you into that mess in Houston was because you were pregnant.''

''Oh, that . . .''

The way Courtney dropped her gaze, then lowered her head, made Kendall's mouth go dry. ''That *is* what you said, isn't it, that you were going to have a baby?''

A tear trickled down Courtney's heavily made-up face. ''Ellis said you wouldn't keep quiet if it was just him and me getting into trouble.'' She raised her mascara-smudged eyes. ''I'm so sorry, Kenny. He said that since you'd never been in trouble you'd just get a slap on the wrist and everything would be fine.''

Anger like Kendall had never known roiled around inside her. The betrayal she had felt five years ago was nothing compared to what she felt now. At least then she'd thought she was protecting an innocent baby. Courtney had deliberately lied to her to keep herself and Ellis from going to prison.

''I won't sit here and lecture you, Corky,'' Kendall said, snatching up her keys and standing. ''And I'll try not to judge you. But when you decide to stop Ellis from hurting more people, maybe I'll be able to forgive you. I just hope you don't wait too long.'' Fighting back the tears, she stormed out to the Suburban, then pulled into the flow of late afternoon traffic.

She told herself she wasn't going to cry. She told herself she was better off without Courtney in her life. She told herself a lot of other things.

But she did cry. And she felt so very alone.

Between missing the children and her problems with Jake and Courtney, Kendall would have found it easy to fall into a deep state of despair over the next several days if it hadn't been for all the work involved in redecorating a house the size of the Sentell place. Things

were going well, with the upstairs rooms coming together much faster than she'd anticipated. Before her
trip to Fort Worth, she had taken the children shopping.
She thought it best to start upstairs, and since they'd
be gone, she wanted them to have as much say as
possible in choosing things for their rooms. She missed
them desperately. And, despite her resolve to put Courtney out of her mind, her heart, and her life, she continued to worry about her.

Even the relationship between Jake and herself had
to be put on the back burner. They were like strangers
living under the same roof. They were cordial and considerate of each other during the evenings, although
Kendall made sure they were never in the same room
for very long. Typically, during the day they rarely saw
each other, and when they did, they were far too busy
to talk about anything except progress on the house and
to exchange tidbits of information about the kids. Jake,
more often than not, was distracted by work. A car
theft ring had crept into his town, taking up all his time,
a blessing in disguise for which Kendall was grateful.

To top things off, she'd lost her purse. She remembered having it with her in Fort Worth, but when she
called the Tejas Cafe asking about it, the manager told
her that no one had turned it in. Her only stroke of
luck was that she had no credit cards and all she'd lost
was ten dollars and some change. Her temporary driver's license would have been another worry if she
hadn't returned home to find that her permanent driver's
license had come in the mail that very day.

Working each day from sunrise to midnight, she fell
exhausted into bed in the wee hours of the morning.
She called the children every day with reports on how
their rooms were coming along; she hung up each time

both happy and depressed that they were having a wonderful time without her.

The brightest spot in her life was her growing friendship with Leza. Where the pregnant woman got her energy, Kendall didn't know, but she was there every morning shortly after Jake left.

Before her marriage to Jared, Leza had been director of visual merchandising at Randolph's, the largest and finest department store in Rosemont. A glorified title for a window dresser, Leza laughingly told Kendall. Still, her background and experience had earned her a reputation for having an eye for detail and she was considered one of the best interior decorators by the elite of Rosemont and her native Odessa. She was more than happy to help Kendall breathe new life into her brother-in-law's house. She'd offered to help Jake redecorate in the past, but he'd never been interested—until now.

Leza usually went home by mid-afternoon so she could be there when the triplets woke up from their naps. Today, though, Maggie had run her off after catching her on her hands and knees scrubbing the same floor Maggie had scrubbed the day before. Since Jared was away on business, Leza decided to come back and go over a few details with Jake. In the meantime, Jake had called home to say he'd be late, not to hold supper for him.

"So far," Leza said, placing both hands at the small of her back and stretching, "this is my very favorite room."

Kendall smoothed the down-filled comforter gracing the king-size bed, then stepped back to admire their handiwork. "It is beautiful," she said, letting her gaze sweep the guest room appreciatively. They had outdone themselves in this room. The overall effect was a soft ice blue so pale that if it weren't for the various shades of blue in the wallcovering and the matching draperies, comforter, and throw pillows, it would have looked cool-white and serene and so very romantic.

A soft moan drew her attention to Leza. She was at her friend's side in seconds. 'Are you all right?''

Leza held on to Kendall's arm and accepted her help to the bench at the foot of the bed. "Yes." She took a deep breath. "These stupid pains are beginning to be a pain."

"I'll call the doctor—''

"No," Leza said, stopping her. "It's okay now. This happened with the triplets. False labor, and it was so embarrassing being sent home three times," she explained, standing. "Don't look so worried. I have better than a week to go. Do you know how much work we can get done in that amount of time?" She was teasing now, and Kendall wasn't sure whether to go along or insist on getting her to the hospital. "Honest, Kendall. I know true labor from false. Help me get these old drapes and bedspread downstairs before Jake gets home. I want him to get the full effect of what we've done."

"Where is everybody?" Jake called from downstairs.

Leza looked at Kendall, then at the heap of fabric lying at her feet. "You distract him while I get these in the closet."

Kendall was just as anxious to see Jake's reaction to the new decor, but she had reservations about leaving Leza alone.

"Go on," Leza insisted, giving her a gentle shove toward the door. "Just give me a few minutes, then bring him up."

Kendall didn't seem to have a choice and did as she was told. She found Jake in the kitchen and smiled at the familiar sight of his broad shoulders and nicely rounded backside standing in front of the open refrigerator.

"I thought you were going to grab a bite at Mrs. Dean's boarding house tonight." She almost laughed aloud when he started like a guilty child at the sound of her voice. Apparently he hadn't heard her coming down the stairs.

He took the fried chicken leg out of his mouth. "Mrs. Dean said if I couldn't get there on time, I could take myself through the first drive-through window I came to. Heartless old woman."

"Kendall!"

They both turned toward the sound of Leza's voice coming from upstairs. Jake reacted immediately. He bounded up the stairs, just seconds ahead of Kendall. They found Leza doubled over at the head of the stairs, bracing herself against the banister.

"Guess I was wrong," she said through the pain. "This is it. My water just bro—" Another pain doubled her over.

Jake seemed rooted to the spot, just three steps away from his sister-in-law. Kendall passed him to put her arm around Leza's shoulders.

"When was the last pain?"

"About two seconds ago." Leza gave her a wan smile. "Sorry. Just after you left me."

Kendall glanced down at Jake, still standing immobile on the steps. "Jake," she said, having to repeat herself when he didn't respond. "Get her to the car while I call Maggie. She'll have to get hold of Jared."

The sound of her voice penetrated his stupor, but still he didn't look quite himself as he scooped Leza into his arms and descended the stairs.

The phone call took only a few seconds. Kendall

quickly grabbed a pillow off her bed and a blanket out of the linen cabinet, then hurried out the back door. Thankfully, Jake had removed the third-row bench seat from the Suburban several days before to allow Kendall and Leza room to haul drapery rods and wallpaper and other decorating items. He'd lowered the tailgate and Kendall heard him speaking to Leza, lying in the cargo space, as she approached.

"Where's Jared?"

"Business trip," Leza said between pants. "Corpus Christi."

"Damn." Kendall had never heard him sound so rattled. "How the hell could he leave town at a time like this?"

Both women heard the censure in his voice, but it was Kendall who tried to calm him. "Jake," she said, laying a quieting hand on his arm. "With twins, a week one way or the other isn't unusual. Everything's going to be all right."

Jake looked at Kendall. She'd never seen pure terror this close before. Then he jerked his gaze back to Leza.

"Don't worry. I'll take care of everything." He sounded strange, almost frantic. "It'll be okay. Just don't die." It was a prayerful whisper.

At that moment Kendall realized he was reliving another time, another pregnancy and labor. She was almost thankful for the pain that took Leza's attention away from Jake. Again she laid her hand on Jake's arm. She had to take control. He was in no emotional shape to drive.

"Give me the keys, Jake," she said, forcing eye contact when he hesitated. "You'll be more help back here with Leza than driving." She wasn't sure what she expected him to do, but she breathed a sigh of relief when he climbed into the cargo space with Leza. Kendall closed the tailgate, then got behind the wheel.

Under normal driving conditions, town was less than twenty minutes away, the hospital maybe thirty. She prayed they would make it in time.

In the back, Leza let out a soft cry of pain. "I don't think we're going to make it," she managed to say. "They're coming faster, harder now. . . ."

Kendall looked in the rearview mirror and her eyes locked with Jake's. Clear and gray, they were free of the fear she'd seen in them just moments ago. Thank God he'd gotten hold of himself.

He rolled up his sleeves and gave Leza a warm and reassuring smile. "It'll be okay, Leza. I promise." He sounded strong and sure.

Kendall breathed a prayer of relief.

"Kendall'll get us there in one piece, and I'm an old hand at this." Again he glanced up at Kendall's reflection in the mirror, then back to Leza. "Just tell that ugly husband of yours that I get to name my nieces."

ELEVEN

Jake checked in on Leza one last time, then closed the door. Turning, he immediately sought Kendall's sleeping form curled up on the slick vinyl piece of utilitarian furniture that masqueraded for a sofa in the hospital's third-floor waiting area. She'd refused to rest until Leza was settled in for the night. Then it had taken less than two minutes, literally, for her to drift off.

He rubbed the muscles of his neck, then stretched the kinks out of his tired, aching back. Delivering babies was hard work, especially in cramped quarters. He couldn't remember the last time he'd been this tired, or this happy. Again he looked at Kendall, remembering the confidence he'd seen in her eyes when they realized they wouldn't make it to the hospital.

He'd almost lost it back at the house. So many memories had come crashing in on him. Thank God Kendall had been there to gently but firmly guide him back to the task at hand. With her behind the wheel, they'd arrived safely at the emergency room door just as his second niece decided to make her entrance into this world.

Kendall sighed in her sleep, the sound drawing Jake to her side. Her eyes fluttered open. "Is Jared here yet?" she asked through a sleepy yawn.

Jake sat next to her. "Not yet," he answered, unobtrusively lifting her head onto his lap. "He should be here any minute. Rest while you can."

She didn't argue or try to move away and in seconds she was dozing again. Jake rested his head against the wall to wait for his brother. They'd called Maggie again while the doctor examined Leza. She had gotten in touch with Jared and said he would be on the next flight out of Corpus Christi and should be in Rosemont no later than two that morning. The clock down the hall said it was two-thirty, but Jake would have sworn it was later.

Kendall stirred and brought her hand up to his knee. He stared at the slender fingers, remembered how they had caressed his cheek just a few short days ago. Without considering the consequences, he took her hand in his, something he'd wanted to do since the first time he'd seen her. Suddenly he was weary of all the mind games they'd been playing ever since that fateful night on the stairs. He'd taken Brad's advice by taking it slow and easy, trying to show her how he felt and that he was ready to stop living in the past. The time for showing was over; it was time to say it, plain and simple.

A loud footfall coming from the elevator signaled Jared's arrival. He looked harried and scared. Jake held his index finger to his lips and motioned at Kendall.

"Leza and your daughters are all fine and resting," he whispered. He figured that was all Jared really wanted to know right now. He was right.

Jared flashed him a tired but happy smile, then sat in the chair next to the sofa. "I saw Dr. Lauck in the elevator. He said you delivered my babies."

"A sheriff's work is never done." Jake gave his brother a weary grin. "I was there; Leza did all the work." His hand deserted Kendall's to absently stroke her hair. "I figured you'd want to stay the night, so you're footing the bill for two semiprivate rooms."

"With what you saved me on labor and delivery rooms, I think I can afford it." Again they exchanged smiles. Money had ceased to be a problem for either of them years ago. "Well," Jared said, his gaze lowering to Jake's hand, still caressing Kendall's hair. "I guess this ties things up between us."

Jake knew he was tired, but Jared's last remark was lost on him. "Sorry, you lost me on that."

Jared stretched his long legs out in front of him and crossed his booted ankles. "The way I tally it, this makes five little Sentells for me against your five." Again his gaze drifted to Kendall, sleeping with her head resting on Jake's thigh. "You thinking about going one better?"

Healthy competition between Jake and his twin had kept them sharp over the years. The number of children they each had fathered became a standing joke from the day Leza learned she was expecting twins after presenting Jared with triplets just two short years earlier. Jared had been pretty smug about accomplishing in three short years what it had taken Jake seventeen to do.

He fought back the instinct to fear for Kendall. "If that's what Kendall wants and needs." It felt good to finally say what he'd felt in his heart for weeks. "You okay with that?" They both knew Jake wasn't asking Jared's permission. Jake also knew that it had taken

Jared a while to warm to Kendall and the idea that she had served time.

"If she's what you want and need." Jared was rarely at a loss for words, but he seemed to be now. "You stood beside me all those years I was alone. Then Leza came into my life and you knew I'd be okay. Since Becky . . ." His voice broke. "You've been alone long enough, Jake. Kendall's made the difference for you and the kids. I'm happy for you."

Suddenly Jake felt a great sense of relief wash over him. In his heart he knew if it had come down to a choice between his brother and Kendall, he'd have chosen Kendall and then prayed that Jared would come around. He was grateful his brother hadn't put him in that position.

Jared dragged his feet up under him and stood. "Thanks for taking care of my lady, big brother," he said. "I think you'd better get yours home and in bed."

"For once, little brother, I think I'll take your advice." Jake was less than five minutes older than Jared, but the "big brother–little brother" designation had seen them through a lot of years.

Gently rousing Kendall, Jake waited, red-faced, while she filled Jared in on all that had happened, even to the length of expounding on Jake's midwifery skills.

When he could take it no longer, he put his arm around her trim waist and propelled her toward the bank of elevators at the end of the hall, leaving Jared smiling smugly at their backs.

The trip from town back to the house passed far too fast to suit Kendall. The moment Jake slid behind the wheel of the Suburban, he reached over to gently pull her across the seat to sit next to him. The gesture had been so spontaneous, had felt so right, that she didn't protest, not even when he placed his arm around her, eased her closer still. Somehow she knew that tonight they both needed the physical contact. What she didn't know was what to expect next.

On the back porch, Jake held the door open for her. A mid-April breeze kicked up, mingling the fresh clean smell of honeysuckle and gardenia and freshly mown grass with the masculine scent that was uniquely Jake Sentell. She reached inside for the light switch, only to have Jake's hand cover hers. He stood behind her. The heat from his lean, muscular body radiated across the space between them to inflame her without so much as a touch.

She turned then, raising her gaze to meet his. Even in the moonlit darkness, she saw his features clearly. Dark and lean, he came as close to perfection as any man she'd ever known. High cheekbones above a firm jaw and chin lent his suntanned and rugged good looks an air of quiet authority. But it was the provocative swell of his lips that captured and held her spellbound. The hand that had covered hers came to rest on her cheek, the other one claimed the gentle curve of her waist. Was she imagining the tenderness in the hard angle of his jaw, the passion glowing in the shadowed gray depths of his eyes?

"Jake," she said, her whisper sounding husky and seductive even to her. "What are you doing?" She didn't want anything else to pass between them that would cause her more pain or regret.

He didn't answer right away. Instead, one hand slipped behind her neck, his fingers splaying through her unbound hair to firmly cup the back of her head. "Before we go any further," he finally said, "I want to know how we stand."

"I'd like to know that myself." For one of the few

times in her life, Kendall resorted to evading an issue. She didn't expect him to let her get away with it, but he did.

After a moment he said, "I'm sorry I hurt you."

She thought they had settled that, but wouldn't insult either of them by pretending not to know what he was talking about. "How can I convince you that you didn't?"

"I don't mean physically." When she didn't answer, Jake went on, "Be as honest as you've always been, Kendall. Tell me how you feel about me. No games. No waiting to see what my next move will be. Just the truth."

The way he said her name always weakened her resolve to remain aloof and unaffected. Now was no exception, only this time it was coupled with the knowledge that her future—their future, if there was to be one—depended solely on her answer.

"I never believed in love at first sight," she said, feeling her heart thumping wildly inside her chest, "until you walked into your office with your nose buried in my file." She'd gone this far, she might as well say it so there would be no chance for a misunderstanding. "I love you, Jake." Her fear dissolved the instant he drew her closer to rest his cheek against her forehead.

"Which is exactly what I saw in your eyes afterward that night," she heard him say. "And I wasn't ready then to admit that I love you, too." He fell silent a moment. "I thought I had used you to blot out the guilt and pain I've lived with for my part in Becky's death."

Kendall was astounded. Why hadn't she seen it before? It wasn't just that the date was the anniversary of Becky's death. It was that he had failed to protect his wife. Now that she thought back, she remembered

Leza's mentioning that Becky wouldn't hear of any kind of permanent sterilization for either of them, even at her doctor's urging. What torture it must have been for Jake all these years to have lived with the knowledge that *if* only he'd taken the responsibility upon himself his wife might still be alive. Then there was his torment over Becca's birthday party. *The day his wife had died.* Silently Kendall cursed herself for adding to his pain—and for judging him so harshly for never having planned a birthday celebration for his daughter.

"Jake—"

"Let me finish, Kendall." She heard in his voice the need to say aloud what was in his heart. "Tonight made me see things clearly for the first time. No one was to blame for Becky's death. She had the best doctor, the finest delivery room staff, the best of everything that was planned right down to the minute. Earlier tonight Leza had you and me and nothing else. Now Jared has his wife and two beautiful, healthy daughters. Some things can't be explained or rationalized." He drew a deep, soul-cleansing breath. "It's been a long time coming, but I know how lucky I am to have my boys and Becca." He released her to look down into her misting eyes. "And now, to have found you seems almost too good to be true."

She couldn't speak for the tears pressing to fall. She had dreamed but had never thought to hear him say the very things he'd just said to her.

Jake tilted her chin upward so that he could see her face clearly. "If I go inside with you now, I won't settle for anything less than forever."

"Neither will I." She raised her face for his kiss, a kiss so achingly tender that it stole away every ounce of willpower she possessed.

Jake broke the contact and rested his forehead against

hers. "You make me feel everything I thought I'd never feel again," he whispered, his voice low and husky. He closed the door behind them, shutting out the rest of the world as he held his hand out to her.

The instant her fingers touched his, Kendall knew that from this moment forward, she was no longer alone, that she would follow wherever he led. His words had given her everything—hope, a dream, the love she'd always wanted and never received. And she wanted to give the same to him. Taking his hand, she started for her room.

Jake stopped her by tugging her into his embrace. "No," he whispered, taking the lead up the stairs. When he paused before the door to the guest room, her old insecurities came flooding back.

She hesitated. "Jake, are you sure?"

He kissed her again, this time lingering to trace the inside of her lower lip with his tongue before saying, "You've changed my world, Kendall Jamison. Now I want to do the same for you." His hands caressed her shoulders, traveled down the length of her arms to take her hands in his. "You're my life now," he said, quieting her fears. "I won't let anyone stand between us. Not even Becky." This time when his lips claimed hers, she knew beyond a doubt that he was finally free of the ghosts, of the guilt.

"Jake," she said on a whisper, not wanting to say or do anything that might take away from the moment. Still, she knew that one of them had to be sensible this time. "I'm not .. . I mean . . ." she stammered. Then, "The last time, when I wasn't pregnant, I saw no reason to see a doctor. I'm still not protected."

At first he looked somewhat chagrined that he hadn't thought that far in advance. Then he tilted her chin upward. "That's my department," he reassured her with a lingering kiss. "Don't go away."

She watched him disappear into Josh's room to return several seconds later. In his hand she saw a foil strip of condoms. The surprise must have shown on her face, because Jake grinned.

"Good old Rosemont High," he said. "When Josh came home with these at the beginning of the school year, we sat down and had our man-to-man talk. I don't know whether to be worried or relieved that they're all still here."

At the moment, Kendall didn't want to talk about Josh. "Knowing Josh, I don't think I'd worry," she said, coming up on her toes to nibble at Jake's ear. He groaned and held her tighter.

Opening the door, he stood beside her in silence and surveyed for the first time the changes she'd made in the master bedroom. She felt her heart rate accelerate. Would it be enough to keep the past at bay?

At last he turned to her. "Blue" was all he said, letting his hand wander the length of her back. "I should have known."

She didn't remember moving into the room or removing their clothes, but at last they stood in each other's arms beside the bed.

Jake was everything she remembered. Muscular and powerfully built, his body could have been that of a man many years his junior. She couldn't resist touching him a moment longer.

She felt the tensile strength of his body against hers, saw the struggle for control in his slow, uneven intake of breath when her fingers trailed across the firm plane of his stomach, then back up to tease his nipples. It thrilled her to see them harden, the same way hers responded to his touch. Her eyes closed and she was able to feel every nerve ending in her body awaken beneath his seeking hands and mouth. Her skin felt fevered everywhere he touched.

She quivered at the powerful emotion exploding between them, emotion that was much more than desire alone. At last, when they could hold back no longer, they sank to the bed in a tangle of heated flesh and limbs. Jake moved over her, taking his time to stoke the fire that was already burning deep inside her.

Rising up, he gazed down at her. His eyes, now darkened with passion, took in every detail of her face, then her body. "Beautiful," he whispered, accepting the myriad kisses she bestowed on his chin and neck. "So perfect," he said with a rough moan, his hands moving over her.

She knew her body pleased him, but where she had wanted to pleasure him, he took away her will with words of love and passion and with kisses that trailed from her closed eyelids to her throat and breasts and lower across the flat contour of her stomach . . . and lower still.

When his lips left her inner thigh and found the center of her womanhood, she cried out his name. Exquisitely attuned to her needs and responses—a sigh, a subtle shifting of her body—Jake grew bolder by positioning himself between her thighs.

And in the first thrust of his body into hers she knew that they had claimed each other forever. And forever with Jacob Sentell was all she would ever need.

Throughout the remainder of the early morning hours, they loved each other. They took turns in taking the lead, until finally Kendall, sated and more content than she'd thought humanly possible, snuggled alongside Jake with her head on his shoulder. Watching the morning sun steal into the room and fall across his body, barely concealed beneath the sheet, she felt her love for him fill her so that it was a physical pain. God, she loved him. She felt it in her heart and knew it in her head, which, at the moment, was driving other parts of her body crazy.

In sleep, his features lost their hardness, the defensiveness she suspected had been a part of him for a long, long while. She had done that for him, and the knowledge was almost as satisfying as their lovemaking. Rising up, she lost the battle to resist kissing his one and only dimple, somehow remembering that Jared also had only one. Jake stirred and she smiled.

"Since Jared's dimple is in his right cheek," she said, nipping his chin, "and yours is in your left, does that still make you identical twins?"

Jake opened one eye to look at her. "Where did that come from?"

Kendall couldn't help laughing. She felt good; she felt loved; she felt giddy. "I honestly don't know. You're probably used to people asking you silly questions like—" She couldn't believe what was going through her mind. Sensible, straight-talking Kendall was having risqué thoughts.

A broad, knowing smile eased across Jake's face. "Like what?"

"Nothing." Embarrassed, she dropped her head to his chest. She felt his hand on her head, reveled in the feel of his fingers slipping through her hair. His heart beat strong and steady beneath her ear.

"Come on, sweetheart. You can ask me anything."

She raised her head and grinned. "I was just wondering if you're identical in every way."

'Yeah," he drawled sleepily. "I guess we are, except that I have an inch or so on him."

She rose on one elbow and eyed him with thinly

disguised skepticism. "If I remember right, Jared's a little taller . . . than . . ." She felt the heat of color rising in her face.

Jake's grin was as endearing as it was mischievous. "Now, I ask you, did either of us say anything about height?"

Apparently she wasn't the only one capable of risqué thoughts at such an early hour. She gave him a playful slap on his shoulder. "I didn't know I was getting involved with a degenerate," she teased, letting her fingers dally in the dark and crisply curling hair that covered his chest. "Don't tell me you two actually compared . . . I mean measured . . . ?"

Jake laughed. "Well, we were young and competitive about everything. You know how brothers are."

The lilt in his voice hit Kendall full force, only because it reminded her of how much she'd missed as a child, that she had so few childhood memories, which, in turn, reminded her of Courtney's betrayal. "No, I can't say that I do."

"Maybe not," he said, gathering her close and caressing her bare shoulder, then the length of her arm, "but surely you and Courtney shared things just as silly."

Kendall shouldn't have been surprised that he had pieced it all together, but she was speechless.

"It's okay, sweetheart. You don't have to tell me anything you'd rather not. I'm a pretty good listener, though, when you're ready."

"You're pretty good at reading between the lines, too."

"It's my job."

"Well," she said, sitting up, "part of my job is cooking, and I'm starved." She reached for her pillow to cover herself, but Jake took it and, with a grin, stuffed it under his head. Kendall managed to grab the sheet. "How do pancakes with oodles and oodles of thick gooey syrup and sausage and bacon and *real* milk, not skim, sound to you?"

Jake feigned shock. "Why, Kendall. I'm surprised at you. No whole-grain cereal or bran muffins or fresh fruit, and what about all that cholesterol?" he asked, tugging at the sheet.

She laughed and swatted his hand away. "When the kids get home, we'll get back to setting all sorts of good examples. For now, let's indulge."

His other hand found her breast beneath the sheet. "Indulge?" he whispered, repositioning her to his advantage. "I like the way you think."

Another hour passed before they made it downstairs. They laughed and talked and worked together to prepare a breakfast that would have any self-respecting doctor quaking in his Italian loafers. Never had Kendall felt so at peace, or so loved. If only her mother were alive to share her happiness. Or if Courtney . . .

"Why the sad face?"

She glanced across the table to see Jake's worried expression. Although he'd obviously put enough together to know about Courtney, there was still much he didn't know about her. Like her relationship with Ellis. Was it fair to keep so much of her past a secret from him? No, it wasn't fair, but now wasn't the time.

"Sad? I was trying to be sexy," she said, pulling her lips into what she hoped was in irresistible pout.

Jake pushed back his plate, then came to stand behind her chair. Both hands on her shoulders, he gently massaged. "Know what I want to do now?" he said, leaning down close to her ear.

"No," she answered, not wanting anything at the

moment except to keep him beside her. "But I hope it involves me."

His hand slid past her shoulders, down the front of her robe. "I haven't been skinny-dipping since . . . since . . . I don't remember when." By this time he'd managed to untie her sash. "We might not have this opportunity again. You game?"

"I'm game for anything you can think up." Kendall stood, turning into the welcoming embrace that was becoming all too addictive.

"Have I mentioned how perfect you are?"

His hands moving over her body made it almost impossible for her to form a coherent thought. "I'm too tall," she answered in a whisper, beginning to find it difficult to think clearly.

"No, you're just right," he said against her lips. To emphasize his point, he ran his hand over her bottom, pressing her intimately against him. "See. Besides, small women make me nervous. You know, awkward and kind of bullish." Now he took her hand and started out the back door.

"But Becky was small. . . ."

"Yes, she was small and fragile, more than a little dependent. All that made me feel like a man, her protector, which was what I needed in the beginning. But you . . ." He stopped and cupped her face in his large hands. "You, Kendall Leigh Jamison," he said on a husky whisper, "are woman enough to take me on your terms, my terms, any way you'll have me." He kissed her on the tip of her nose. Then, slipping her robe off her shoulders, he stepped out of his jeans and swooped her into his arms. "And right now you're going to have me in the pool," he said, striding across the yard.

No sooner were the words spoken than they landed

in the deep end of the pool. They came up laughing and kissing and touching and would have ended up making love in the mid-morning sun if a startled "Oh" hadn't interrupted.

Looking up, Kendall saw Vanna Tyler standing near the edge of the yard. With all the splashing and cavorting, it was no wonder they hadn't heard her arrive.

"I'm . . . I'm sorry," the girl sputtered. Her startled eyes darted from them to their discarded clothes, then back. "I thought Brad might be home for spring break."

Jake shielded Kendall's body with his own. "No, Vanna. He has a job that keeps him in Austin," he said to the girl's retreating back. A few seconds passed before they heard the slamming of a car door.

"Oh, Jake," Kendall said over the roar of Vanna's engine, "what sort of trouble will this cause you?"

Jake laughed and pulled her against his body. The man was amazing. He was still aroused. "No wonder I love you," he said, drawing her lip between his and sucking gently. "All you can think of is how this will affect me."

"Seriously, Jake." She was having a difficult time concentrating on the problem at hand. "I don't know her very well, but from all you and Brad said about her family, isn't it logical that she'll go straight to her mother and grand—"

He silenced her by kissing her again, this time longer and harder. "The only logical thing I have on my mind right now is making you as hot for me as I am for you."

Which took a sinfully short amount of time to accomplish.

Jake sat at his desk, reading the same file for the fourth time. His mind hadn't been on work from the time he walked into his office after dropping Kendall off at the hospital to visit with Leza. All he wanted to do was play hooky, go back and pick up Kendall, take her home, and make love over and over and over. . . .

Even now, just the thought of her in his bed quickened his blood.

He leaned back and smiled, ignoring the irritating squeak his worn old chair always made. He'd forgotten just how good life could be, and he couldn't wait for the kids to get home so he and Kendall could tell them they were getting married.

"Are you finished with the reentry applicant files?" Stephanie Britt asked, interrupting his erotic little daydream.

Jake glanced up at the sound of his secretary's voice. Young, in her early twenties, Stephanie had come to work for him just a year ago. He didn't make it a practice to hire his friends' kids, but Willie Britt had asked the favor in the hope that it would keep his only daughter away from a bad crowd she'd started hanging out with. Things had worked out for everyone concerned. Stephanie was back in school, taking night courses at Rosemont Junior College, Willie was his cheerful self again, and Jake had the best secretary he'd ever employed. And in the short time she'd been there, she'd made herself indispensable to him, earning the nickname Radar early on because of her uncanny knack for knowing when Jake needed something.

Today, however, he'd requested the latest reentry applications when he hit the door. He had a new housekeeper to find.

"Yep," he said, closing the last of the files on his desk. "And here's my list of the ones I'd like to interview." He wanted the new housekeeper to be a surprise, but, of course, Kendall would have the final say.

Stephanie took the files and the list and started to leave. At the door, she stopped and turned around. "Sheriff."

Jake looked up, seeing that something was on her mind. "Yes?" Was he imagining a rosy glow creep across her fair features?

"It may not be my place to say so," she began, "but I'm really happy for you."

Jake felt a wide grin split his face. "You're amazing," he said. "Or am I just that transparent?"

Stephanie returned his smile. "A little of both, I'm sure. And Daddy's mentioned that you haven't been by his place in a long time," she said, reaching for the door. "Anyway, I've only met Miss Jamison a few times, but I think you've got a real winner there. I hope you'll be very happy."

"Thanks, Radar." Jake nodded at the files in her hands. "And make this a priority. I don't want Kendall to have anything on her mind except planning our wedding."

TWELVE

Sunday in the sleepy little town of Rosemont, where the people were friendly and down to earth, had come to be Kendall's favorite day of the week. Today was even more special because she felt beautiful and content and loved. Part of the reason was that Jake had spent every moment possible with her since the night Leza gave birth. He went to work late, came home for leisurely lunches, and ended his workday earlier and earlier. He'd even gone shopping with her one afternoon, and together they'd picked out the lovely suit of palest blue linen that, according to Jake, matched the color of her eyes to a T.

And to her, Jake was the most handsome man in the small community church in a navy pin-striped suit, crisp white shirt, and a very fashionable tie Kendall had talked him into buying. Only one other man came even close to being competition, and that was Jared. Of course, Leza would have argued the point had she been able to attend church with the rest of them. But she was home with her babies, leaving Kendall free to rank the men any way she wanted.

During the service, the theme of which, was "Judge not, that ye be not judged," she'd looked up more than once to find Jake watching her. At times she found it hard to believe how much he loved her. Still, one look into those ash-colored eyes left no doubt that it was so.

Later, standing in the churchyard with Jared, who was the epitome of the proud father sharing photos of his newborn daughters, Kendall glanced up to see Mrs. Tyler and Marianne Prescott-Tyler approaching Jake across the way. Things looked cordial enough at first, but Kendall easily read the displeasure in his face, saw it in the rigid way he held his body.

She touched Jared's arm. "I'll be right back," she told him. The trio was too engrossed in what Kendall suspected was an argument to hear her approach.

"I've done some checking, Sheriff, and know all about that woman's past and how you found her," she heard the elder Mrs. Tyler saying. "I won't stand idly by and allow any more of the reentry program's money to be spent supporting a lifestyle I feel is sinful."

Kendall cringed at the onslaught of condemning words, but she felt sorry for the woman when Jake's features tightened with a scowl. She prayed Mrs. Tyler would have the good sense to back off.

"That woman's name is Kendall Jamison, and she's the best thing that ever happened to my family. And to me." He pinned her with an angry glare. "As for my sinful lifestyle, Mrs. Tyler, the only thing I have to ask forgiveness for is listening to your unfounded slander."

"Unfounded?" Marianne stepped forward. "My Vanna saw the two of you naked as the day you were born, cavorting outside in broad daylight. What if one of your children had found you instead?"

"My children have been with their grandparents for

the past week." His voice was low, on the verge of threatening.

Kendall sensed a presence beside her, felt Jared's hand at her waist. The cavalry had moved in for support.

"Mrs. Tyler," Jared addressed the woman, guiding Kendall to stand next to Jake. She heard the barely controlled anger in his voice, sensed it in the stiff carriage of his body. "Marianne." He removed his hand only when Jake eased his arm around her.

Kendall wasn't going to just stand by dumbstruck and let Jake take the flak alone. "If Vanna'd had the good manners to call before showing up uninvited, all this could have been avoided," she said to both women. "And you have to know that Jake would never do anything to embarrass or hurt his children."

Mrs. Tyler, dressed in a paisley drop-waist dress of green jersey, puffed up like a great toad. "I find it admirable that you would defend your lover, Miss Jamison, but I refuse to condone this kind of behavior, especially when it involves one of our most trusted and respected elected officials."

She turned again to Jake. "I'm calling a special meeting of the finance committee, Sheriff. The good people of Rosemont should know what their donations to the reentry program are paying for. You'll be notified. I, for one, have no intention of contributing another dime as long as Miss Jamison is living under your roof."

Before Jake could counter, she turned on her heel and marched off, a very stiff-backed Marianne following closely behind. The only positive thing about the altercation was that no one else had been close enough to overhear.

Once they were gone, Kendall felt her bravado wither. "Oh, Jake," she said, "I'm so sorry."

"You have no reason to apologize." His voice still held its angry edge. "And I'll be damned if I'll let those two stand in judgment over you."

She reached out to put her hand on his arm. The muscles there were taut with tension. "That doesn't concern me, but putting your program in jeopardy does."

"The Tylers are influential in Rosemont," Jared interrupted, "but they aren't the end-all."

Kendall appreciated Jared's support for both Jake and herself. "I know," she said, "but, Jake, this isn't Houston or Dallas. No matter how cosmopolitan Rosemont residents might like to think they are, they're still small-town people with 1950s ideas about certain things. If Mrs. Tyler can use this to influence others to withdraw their support, she can cause you trouble in other ways." She couldn't believe how scared she was for Jake.

Before the entire congregation, Jake gathered her in his arms. "It's okay, sweetheart. I've dealt with these people all my life. I can handle anything they dare dish out."

"Yeah," she heard Jared say behind her. "And when they mess with my big brother, they mess with me." He sounded so like Timmy that she was tempted to smile, until he added, "The only thing I'm worried about is that election time is just around the corner."

"Oh, Jake," she moaned into the crook of his neck.

She felt his head jerk to one side, then heard Jared meekly say he'd meet them back at the car. She didn't have to see Jake's face to know that he wasn't happy with Jared for mentioning the election.

Drawing back, he smiled. "Those two vipers obviously were too busy plotting their next move to hear the message in today's sermon.'' They were walking toward the parking lot by now, and Kendall felt better when several families stopped to say hello. Surely Mrs. Tyler and her daughter-in-law weren't representative of the entire population of Rosemont.

Finally reaching the Suburban, where Jared already had his boys in their safety seats, Jake asked, ''You up to doing something special after lunch?''

Brooding over trouble, especially trouble that had yet to happen, had never been Kendall's way, and she welcomed the opening to lighten the mood. ''I've heard it called a lot of things, but 'something special'?''

Once again she was rewarded with a seductive smile and a husky, ''Everything I do with you is special. Especially that.''

''Do you two mind?''

They looked over the hood of the Suburban to see Jared grinning at them. ''If you keep that up, I might have to back the Tylers at their meeting,'' he teased.

Jake threw his hat at him and opened the door for Kendall. ''He always was the fence straddler in the family.'' His hat flew back to hit him in the face. ''You'd better be careful, little brother,'' he threatened. ''It's not too late to change your babies' names. How do Prudence and Drusilla sound to you?''

Jared obviously knew when to quit. He held up both hands in surrender. ''If it's all the same to you, we'll stick with Megan and Paige.''

The razzing continued throughout the drive to Summerset Ranch, where Kendall helped with the finishing touches to the Sunday dinner Leza and Maggie had prepared while everyone else went to church. After lunch, Kendall felt like part of the family when Maggie enlisted her help in getting the triplets down for their nap. It was harder getting Leza to lie down and rest, but with two mother hens like Kendall and Maggie hovering over her, she finally gave in.

Basking in the feeling of finally belonging to a real family, Kendall found Jake outside on the veranda. Both he and Jared had discarded their coats and ties. With their feet propped up on the porch railing, they looked relaxed and at peace with the world.

"I'm ready when you are," she said, hating to disturb them but wanting to spend as much time alone with Jake as possible before the children returned home next weekend. She shouldn't have worried, for when Jake looked up, the smile he had for her plainly said that he was just as eager to be with her, too. He stood and in a matter of minutes they'd said their good-byes and were on the road.

During the two-mile drive between the Sentell houses, Kendall did her best to learn what Jake had in mind for the rest of the afternoon, but to no avail. Finally reaching the house, Jake checked on Bob and the pups, then changed into jeans and a well-worn chambray shirt. The faded blue fabric complemented his suntanned coloring, and she gave in to the impulse to run her hands over the soft material that covered his chest. He pulled her to him and kissed her soundly before giving her a twirl for his personal inspection. Kendall opted for an oversized pullover with bold nautical navy and white stripes. The hem hung well past her hips, covering all but the bottom portion of the white leggings she sported. She felt cool and casual and, since Jake had repeatedly refused to tell her where they were going, ready for anything he could come up with for them to do this afternoon.

They headed south on Highway 155, then made numerous turns onto twisting country roads she had no idea even existed. Her only clues to their destination were road signs and billboards announcing that they were nearing Lake Palestine. Dense forest lined each side of the road, and occasionally she would glimpse a flowering dogwood or blooming redbud tree, but it was the abundance of climbing wisteria that delighted her most.

In all the time she'd known Jake, he'd never pressured her to tell him about her past. But today, probably because of the length of time in reaching their destination, Kendall realized that he'd given her several opportunities to tell him about her involvement with the scam in Houston and her relationships with both Ellis and Courtney. Why she was reluctant to bare her soul to him, she wasn't sure, but she couldn't, not yet. He finally pulled off the narrow blacktop road onto a dirt trail and turned off the engine. The trail curved and disappeared into a stand of pines and oaks and hickory trees.

"Close your eyes," he said, getting out and coming to her side of the Suburban.

Taking his proffered hand, she giggled and did as he asked. "What are you up to?"

"What's the matter," he whispered near her ear, "don't you trust me?"

"With my life." She hadn't meant it to sound so serious, and found herself in his embrace. Opening her eyes, she saw his somber face before hers.

"You are my life." A quick kiss and he released her. "Now close your eyes and don't tempt me again."

They moved slowly along the trail, with Jake carefully guiding her. Finally she heard him say, "Okay, sweetheart, open your eyes."

She hadn't realized the main road had been slowly winding upward, and she caught her breath at the panoramic view that stretched before her. From atop a hill in densely forested timber country she saw an open body of water that seemed to go forever. Below her, going down the hillside, was a wooden walkway that meandered toward the water's edge. A short pier led the way to a good-sized boathouse that gave every appearance of basking in the afternoon sun.

She leaned into the warm support of Jake's body behind her. "I've never seen such a beautiful place."

Jake's arms encircled her. "I'm glad you like it," he said. "It's yours."

"Jake, you're not serious." She turned, only to find herself in his arms. "Are you?"

He laughed and turned her to face the opposite direction, where he pointed to a cabin perched upon the plateau between where they stood and the road. "Have I ever lied to you?"

"Of course not," she answered, still unable to believe his generosity.

"I've owned the cabin and the surrounding ten acres for several years now. I come here when things start to crowd in on me and I need to be alone. No one else knows about it, no one at work, not even my kids or Jared."

Suddenly she remembered Leza telling her how he had disappeared after Becky's death, sometimes for days on end. She was hardly aware that they were walking toward the cabin. "Jake, I can't accept this. It's your special place."

"I want to share everything with you. Let me." When he looked at her with love shining in his eyes, she would refuse him nothing. They reached the front door and he unlocked it.

Inside, the light was dim, but she was able to make out one great room with a magnificent rock fireplace and hearth that covered one entire wall. The kitchen was to the rear of the room. A small island bar that served as table and work area separated the kitchen from the living area. An ancient refrigerator hummed noisily to the left of the room and an outdated cook stove hugged the wall to the right of the sink. In the living area she saw two comfortable-looking easy chairs flanking what looked to be a sleeper sofa, several occasional tables, and a massive wardrobe that stood like a silent sentinel in a far corner.

"I know it's a bit rustic, but I've arranged for a contractor to renovate it. He's already been out to look things over, and by the end of next week we'll have new appliances and a bathroom."

"There isn't a bathroom?"

He gave her an affectionate hug. "If you'd rather I didn't renovate," he said through a laugh, "the outhouse is out back and the lake makes a great bathtub."

"I didn't say that," she said quickly, going on inside to look around. *Rustic* was an understatement. No television. No radio. No telephone. Just shelves and shelves of books and magazines and masculine clutter: several rods and reels and more tackle than she'd ever seen in one place; duck decoys, a kerosene lamp, shells and such. Next to the shelves stood a gun rack, complete with a shotgun, a twenty-two rifle, and a handgun. On the floor lay a rolled up sleeping bag, and on wall pegs hung several items of camouflage clothing. Propped in the corner by the door she saw an ax. No one would argue that this was, indeed, a man's hideaway.

"I've spent a lot of time here, mostly trying to get my head straight during bad times." He invited her to sit next to him on the couch. "I know how hard it is to live in the present with the past constantly breathing down your neck.'' He paused, and Kendall knew what was coming.

''Jake.'' She hesitated, unsure of how to say what she was feeling. ''I don't know if I'm ready to share my pain with you. I've put it in the past, and I don't think it'll ever be a problem between us.''

''We wouldn't let it, Kendall, but we'll be getting married soon.'' He held her gaze with his. ''Tell me honestly, what's a wedding without the bride's only living relative being there for her?''

She should have known that Jake's only motive for wanting to know about her past was that he wanted her wedding day to be perfect. No one—not even Momma—had loved her that much.

That seemed to be all it took to open the floodgates of her memories. Starting with her father's desertion, she told Jake of a ten-year-old girl crying herself to sleep each night, wondering what she'd done to make him leave, all the while bargaining with God to send him home and she'd never be bad again.

It was hard to relive those next few years, when Momma, who had never worked outside the home and who had no formal education, wasn't always able to feed them both.

She snuggled deeper into Jake's embrace. ''She loved me, Jake. I know she did, but it was so hard for her to make ends meet. Even at that young age, I knew how frustrated she was so much of the time. I also knew that I was a burden.'' She glanced up and realized the pain she'd suffered as a child had followed her into adulthood. ''Children should never feel that way.'' Her voice broke and she fought back the tears. ''They should be loved. Cherished.''

Jake didn't try to tell her that she had probably mis-understood or that her mother had done the best she could. Instead, he simply held her until she was ready to go on.

"Things started to look up when Momma met Randall Blankenship, although they couldn't legally marry because there had never been a divorce between her and my father." She smiled, remembering what a dear little girl of four Courtney had been, the sister Kendall had always wanted.

For a while, she told Jake, they played at being happy by overlooking Randall's violent outbursts of temper. Then his drinking got worse and the nightmare began—the nightly fights, the yelling, the trips to the emergency room when he'd gone too far in abusing Momma, who fought back only when he vented his wrath on the girls.

Jake pulled her closer when she told him about the car wreck seven years later that claimed Randall's life and left her mother near death for several days. The hardest part was recalling the times she'd sat beside her mother's bed, unable to lessen her pain, listening to her labored breathing while she made Kendall promise to always take care of Courtney.

She held her own tears in check while she related Courtney's tearful pleading to stay with her when the Blankenship sisters came and forced her to go with them back to Dallas. Next she told him of the day Courtney showed up on her doorstep seven years later, again begging Kendall to remember her promise to Momma and let her stay with her. She should have known better than to believe all the stories Courtney told of her aunts' mistreating her. All that mattered was that Courtney was back with her—and that Kendall was finally able to keep her promise to her mother.

"Which brings us to Ellis Trammell?" Jake prompted when Kendall drew a weary breath.

"Which brings us to Ellis Trammell." She wanted to see his face when she told him about Ellis, so she drew back and leaned against the sofa arm. "Courtney and I were having a hard time making ends meet when we saw an ad for helpers for the Little Miss Houston Pageant. We both applied for jobs and were hired on a part-time basis, since we were working full time at Wee Care." She wasn't sure she should or could go on with her story.

"It's okay, sweetheart," Jake said, gently urging her on again. "I think I have it figured out, but you need to say it."

As always, he was right. She nodded and went on. "Ellis was a charmer. Handsome, witty, attentive, everything a woman with a background like mine would be easy prey for." It would have been easier to gloss over her relationship with Ellis, but she needed to say it to be free of it. "Secretly we became lovers, and I foolishly thought we would be married after we saved enough money. What I didn't know was . . ."

"He was putting the same moves on Courtney," Jake finished when she couldn't.

"How could I have been so stupid?" She saw her own pain reflected in Jake's eyes. "I should have known something was wrong when he insisted that we keep our relationship a secret." For the first time ever she thought that he might have used the same ploy on Courtney. How else could he have manipulated them both so easily? Poor Courtney, she thought, empathy for her sister flooding over her. But then she looked into Jake's eyes and remembered that she owed him much more than an explanation. She owed him the truth.

"He used me," she told him plainly. "I thought he truly loved me when he asked so many questions about my family. Now I see that it was just his way of making sure he had an ace in the hole. He wormed all those painful memories out of me, not because he cared, but to learn where my weak spots were. He must have sensed that I would never knowingly be a part of his schemes, so he used my loyalty to Courtney to make sure I'd never say or do anything to hurt him.'' She lowered her eyes. ''Or Courtney and the baby she said she was carrying.''

''I see'' was all he said, pausing to let her regain her composure. ''I have a feeling there's more.''

Remembering that first day in his office when he'd expressly forbidden her to have any contact with Ellis or Courtney, she wasn't sure how he would take the news that she'd visited with her that day in Dallas.

''On my way back from Fort Worth, I stopped at a cafe just outside of Dallas. There, on the door, was a flier about a children's pageant. I couldn't believe he was still getting away with the same scam that sent me to prison, but I couldn't leave without knowing for sure. I called the number and Courtney answered the phone.'' She swallowed, then went on to tell him all that had passed between her sister and herself, including the lie about the baby and how she had stormed out without hearing anymore. She finished with, ''That's probably where I left my purse. Either Courtney has it or someone else walked out with it.'' She hadn't shed a tear, and her insides were paying the price. Her stomach knotted with tension.

This time when she fell silent, Jake closed the gap between them. ''If I could take away the pain, I would,'' she heard him say, and she knew that he meant every word.

''You have, Jake.'' She leaned into the protective circle of his arms. ''You have.''

"I love you, Kendall." Those words so sincerely spoken would have been enough for her, but then he tilted her chin to gaze down into her eyes. "I cherish you."

Every heartache she'd ever suffered became a distant memory. In that moment Kendall knew that he would never hurt her. They sat in silence, watching the afternoon sun slowly bid the day a glorious farewell outside their window, until finally Jake spoke.

"I can't imagine anything lonelier than not having Jared around all these years." He drew back to look at her. "There's no room in our future for unsettled business, sweetheart. You need to make your peace with Courtney. Not for her sake. Not for mine. For your own."

Again she knew he was right, but the wound of learning that Courtney had lied to her, had deliberately chosen Ellis over her, was still too fresh. "I'll think about it" was all she was able to say.

"In the meantime, think about this." Jake's lips on hers had never tasted sweeter, had never promised more, and she lost herself over to the rapture of his body moving over hers as they took each other again to that special place they created together.

THIRTEEN

Kendall glanced at the digital clock on the dashboard, then back at the road in front of her. Ten thirty. The meeting had started thirty minutes ago, but it seemed more like hours.

Earlier that morning when Jake told her he'd rather she didn't attend, she'd respected his wishes and gone about her daily routine as usual, with the exception of a quick trip to the grocery store. She planned a special lunch for just the two of them with the hope that positive thinking would influence the outcome of the meeting. Still, she hadn't been able to keep her mind off what could amount to Jake's future as sheriff of Smithboro County. He'd adamantly refused to listen to her offer to find another job on her own. No one was running her off, he'd sworn. He hadn't said so, but Kendall knew that if the committee insisted he fire her, he would have no compunction about resigning. She didn't want it to come to that and prayed the committee would look past the gossip and see Jake for the upstanding man he had always been. No, she thought with a heavy sensation creeping in to spoil her mood, she *wouldn't* let it come to that.

With her thoughts rambling around inside her head, she turned off the main road onto the lane that led to Cold Creek Ranch, only vaguely noting the solitary vehicle sitting in the roadside park. A few minutes later she pulled into her parking spot at the end of the driveway. A canary yellow BMW sat in Jake's parking place. Glancing toward the backyard, she saw Courtney sitting at the patio table beside the pool.

Forgetting the groceries, Kendall got out of the Suburban and headed toward Courtney, who was standing now. The closer she got, the more worried she became. Courtney was a disheveled mess. Her hair was tousled, her clothes rumpled, and her makeup, especially her mascara, was smudged. But it was the bruise on her cheek and her swollen upper lip that scared Kendall the most.

"Corky, are you okay?"

Courtney stumbled toward Kendall, the tears and words flowing so freely that Kendall couldn't make out what she was saying. She waited for the weeping to stop, then helped her sister back to a chair.

"Now," she began, sitting opposite Courtney, "tell me what happened."

Courtney finally managed to pull herself together. "I shouldn't have come here," she said between sniffles. "But I couldn't go back to Marilyn's and Maxine's. He knows where they live."

"Ellis?" Kendall prompted unnecessarily. She knew exactly who Courtney meant.

Courtney nodded. "Only his real name is Jordan. Jordan Ellis." She sniffed brokenly. "Kenny, he isn't the same man you knew in Houston. He's changed, sick. I'm sure he's going to kill me."

Courtney couldn't have said anything that would have surprised her more. Kendall looked at her sister's tear-stained and bruised face and began to get scared. "Just calm down and tell me what happened," she said, trying to sound more collected than she felt.

Courtney sniffed again and rummaged through her purse. "Things are falling apart in Dallas." Taking out a tissue, she dabbed at her mascara-smudged eyes. Then she handed Kendall another handbag, one she immediately recognized as the one she'd left in the cafe. Obviously Courtney had taken it with her that day. Which answered Kendall's unasked question as to how Courtney had found her.

"Some people have been coming around, asking all sorts of questions about us," Courtney began. "And Ellis is seeing another woman." Again the tears started to flow. "He doesn't even try to hide it anymore. And, Kenny, I'm pregnant . . ." She stopped to raise her gaze to Kendall's. "He . . . he told me to get rid of it, but I couldn't. I *won't*."

Kendall tried to ignore the uneasy feeling growing in the pit of her stomach. "What did you mean when you said he was going to kill you?"

"He threatened me when I refused to have an abortion and told him I wanted out. I'm tired of running, Kenny. Of being alone, even when he's there."

If everything Courtney had said was true and Ellis thought she was somehow a threat to him, Kendall knew he would find a way to stop her from leaving. Murder was clearly a drastic option but one she was sure he wouldn't rule out.

"Courtney, think hard. Is there any way he could know that you and I have been in touch?" Lord, if Ellis had any idea that Courtney was here, Jake's entire family could be in danger. And it was all her fault. If she hadn't let her hurt feelings send her running home that day in Dallas, if she'd turned Ellis in to the authorities without worrying about the consequences for Courtney, none of this would be happening. Now she was caught between saving Jake's career, possibly his family, and saving Courtney from Ellis.

Courtney looked up. "After our fight this morning, he fell asleep and I sneaked out. He must have heard me leaving, because he followed me. I think I lost him before leaving Dallas—"

"Are you sure?" Kendall demanded. "Absolutely sure?"

Courtney looked startled. "I can't be certain, but—"

"You can't stay here," Kendall flatly stated. She came to her feet and hurriedly gathered up Courtney's purse.

Courtney stood also, her face going pale, then rigid with a combination of fear and anger. "You *have* to help me, Kenny. You promised Momma you'd always take care of me."

For the first time Kendall realized how often over the years Courtney had used her promise to their mother to manipulate her. Well, no more. Guilt no longer had a place in her life.

"I'm going to help you, Corky. Not because of some promise from the past, but because you're my sister and I love you." She put her arm around Courtney's waist. "But you have to help yourself, as well. I can't take the chance of Ellis finding you here. I have to get you someplace safe. Someplace no one would ever think . . . I know exactly where to take you." Thinking all the while, she guided her sister toward the Suburban. She'd just bought groceries, so food would be no problem. She'd get Courtney settled, then come home and tell Jake what was going on. She wasn't foolish enough to think she could handle Ellis on her own, especially if he was as desperate as she thought he was. Surely there was something Jake could do to help.

But first things first. She had to do something with Courtney's car, then get her safely to the cabin. Only then could she stop and think.

Jake hadn't known how worried he was until the meeting was over. He couldn't wait to get home and tell Kendall that the committee had decided in his favor. And to ask her to marry him. Sometime that morning he'd realized that although they had spoken openly of sharing their lives together, had even mentioned the wedding, he had never actually asked her the big question. Well, he intended to rectify that oversight the minute he laid eyes on her. But, he thought with a glance at the fuel indicator, he'd better stop and fill up or he'd never make it to the house.

Butch Blackstone was out the door of his country store to pump the gas before Jake could get out of his patrol car. While Butch checked under the hood, Jake went inside to grab a cold soda. He paid Butch's wife for his purchases and was passing the time of day when Butch came back inside.

"Did yer visitor have a hard time follerin' my directions to yer place, Sheriff?" Butch asked.

"Visitor?"

"Yeah," Butch answered. "Purty young thang in a yeller BMW stopped here 'bout ten or so this mornin', wantin' to know how to get to yer place. I figured she was in trouble, considerin' the mess her clothes was in."

Jake wasn't sure what to make of Butch's tale. "Mind if I use your phone?" It was a rhetorical question. He already had the receiver in his hand. The phone rang eight, nine times. Where was Kendall? She was worried about the outcome of the finance committee meeting and had asked him to come straight home afterward. She'd said she was holding a positive thought and would have a surprise waiting for him. He liked her surprises. He felt himself frowning and hung up, trying to ignore the sense of foreboding that was slowly stealing over him.

He said a hasty good-bye to the Blackstones and pulled into his driveway less than ten minutes later. He swore when he saw that the Suburban was gone.

"Kendall," he called from the back steps, knowing the house was empty by the stillness that hung in the air. He glanced around until something on the patio table caught his attention. He thought he recognized it as the purse Kendall had told him about losing the day she'd taken the children to Fort Worth, but he checked it to make sure. Inside he found her wallet. It contained ten dollars and her driver's permit with Cold Creek Ranch listed as her address. How had the purse gotten back?

More important, where was Kendall?

He began a methodical search, first of the pool and patio area, then the house, where, to his relief, he found nothing incriminating. That left the barn. He didn't know whether to be encouraged or disheartened by the discovery of the BMW Butch had mentioned, but at least he had his first real clue.

He fought the urge to break into a run for the patrol car. He slid behind the wheel and grabbed the radio mike. He would be of no use to Kendall if he panicked. It seemed to take forever for the dispatcher to get back to him with the information he'd requested.

"A 1992 BMW registered to Courtney Ellis . . ."

Jake didn't wait to hear more. He knew that he'd

encouraged Kendall to make her peace with her sister, but gut instinct told him that if Courtney was here after all this time, she was in trouble. And Kendall would help her, no matter what.

He turned the key in the ignition and put the car in gear. He wasn't taking any chances. He'd rather look like a fool than—

He wouldn't think that way. Like Kendall, he'd hold a positive thought.

It took a little longer than Kendall remembered to reach the cabin, but then she'd taken two wrong turns and had to backtrack. Finally they were there and Courtney was resting on the sofa while Kendall put away the groceries.

"Cork?" she called softly, not wanting to disturb her if she was sleeping. She couldn't believe how bad Courtney looked. If she could get her hands on Ellis Trammell—or Jordan Ellis or whatever name he was using this year—she wouldn't be responsible for her actions.

"Yes," Courtney answered.

"I'll fix you a steak and salad if you want to freshen up." The steaks had been for Jake's celebration, but she was sure he would understand.

"I'm not hungry, Kenny."

Kendall put down the cast-iron skillet. "When was the last time you ate?" Courtney shrugged, and Kendall sat beside her and took her hand. "You have to eat something. If not for yourself, think about your baby." That got a reaction.

Courtney placed her hand over the slight swell of her stomach. "My baby," she whispered, the awe in her voice touching Kendall deeply. "You're right, but I can cook for myself. Don't you need to get back?"

Kendall quieted her with a motherly pat on the hand. "Yes, I do, but I have time to pan-broil a steak for you. Medium well, if I remember right."

Courtney smiled, then grew solemn. "For what it's worth now, Kenny, I didn't know about you and Ellis back in Houston." She cleared her throat. "And I couldn't tell you that I was seeing him. He said it would be bad for business if the other workers knew about us."

"I know that now, Courtney. He used the same line on me."

"And Kenny . . ."

Kendall had never seen Courtney quite so serious.

"There's something else." She sat up and made eye contact. "I want you to know that the only reason he chose me over you was because you're a stronger person. You have values and morals that he couldn't manipulate." Her voice broke and she couldn't go on.

For a long, awkward silence, the past crept in like a wedge between them until Kendall shoved it aside. "Let's try to put the past behind us and work on tomorrow."

"I'd like that." Courtney gathered her composure, then stood and looked around. "Where's the bathroom?"

Kendall laughed. "If you have to do anything other than splash water on your face, you'll have to go outside."

"You're kidding."

"Would I kid about something as serious as indoor plumbing?"

"Obviously not," Courtney said. "I'll be right back." At the door, she turned. "Thanks, Kendall, for believing me and for helping me when you could have just told me to drop dead."

"What are sisters for?" She watched Courtney go,

for the first time in many years feeling truly at peace with herself—and with Courtney.

Preparing the steak took longer than she anticipated. The cook stove was butane and she was used to an electric range, but at last she had the steak cooking while she created a salad to die for. Suddenly Courtney burst through the front door.

"I thought I saw someone coming through the woods," she all but yelled, trying to catch her breath.

"Calm down," she said, turning the flame out from under the skillet. Kendall didn't want to alarm Courtney any more than was necessary. "It's probably just the contractor Jake hired to make this place more civilized." She thought he'd told her the man wouldn't be here until the end of the week, but maybe she had misunderstood. Suddenly she remembered the car in the roadside park, and her own composure slipped a notch.

She wasn't taking any chances. There were too many guns in the place to be taken off guard. "Lock the door, just in case," she told Courtney and reached for the shotgun.

Courtney didn't have to be told twice, but before she could hit the dead bolt, the door splintered open, knocking her to the floor. Ellis was upon her, dragging her to her feet and calling her vile names as he shoved her backward. She stumbled and fell to the floor again. He was a big man, and the sight of him looming over Courtney put fear in Kendall's heart.

The unloaded shotgun in Kendall's hands was an impotent mass of metal and wood. She screamed for Ellis to back away from Courtney. When he didn't, she grabbed the barrel of the shotgun and swung with all her might. The stock caught him in the jaw, sending him reeling backward through the door. Kendall tried to shove the door closed. Hanging on loosened hinges, it refused to shut, which would have been useless since the doorjamb had splintered upon impact from Ellis's blow.

"Courtney," Kendall yelled shouldering her weight against the door to keep Ellis at bay. "Load the shotgun." Muscles she hadn't used since letting up on her weight training strained.

Dazed, Courtney crawled toward the weapon now lying on the floor at Kendall's feet. "Where are the shells?" she cried, and Kendall saw the panic in her eyes. "There are no shells."

"Yes, there are." She pointed toward the shelf. "There!"

Ellis hit the door again, this time almost sending Kendall sprawling backward. Courtney screamed and cowered behind a chair.

Kendall quickly scanned the room for another weapon, something, anything close enough for her to get her hands on. Only a few feet away, she saw the ax. She had just enough time to wonder if she would have the guts to use it against Ellis when he forced the door open. With no time to second-guess herself, she lunged for the ax and came up with it extended toward him.

He pulled up short, a mixture of surprise and anger on his face, the same face she'd found so alluring a few short years ago. Today his jaw throbbed with rage, his dark eyes darted wildly from her to Courtney, then back. Courtney was right; this was not the same Ellis Trammell she'd known in Houston. This man was crazed.

"Courtney," he said, stepping back without taking his eyes off Kendall, "what have you been telling Kendall?"

Still holding the empty shotgun in her grasp, Courtney edged around the chair to stand behind Kendall.

"The truth," she said through trembling lips. "And she believes me, Ellis. You said she wouldn't, but she believes me."

That seemed to be of grave importance to her, and Kendall realized that Ellis had left his mark on Courtney as well. Where he had used Kendall's loyalty to Courtney to protect himself, he obviously had used Courtney's history of lying to keep her in line.

"Yes, I believe you, Courtney." Kendall couldn't let Ellis undermine their newfound trust in each other.

"You would, you stupid bitch!"

Until this very moment, Kendall hadn't been truly frightened. The glazed look in his eyes, however, warned her that Ellis was capable of much more than name calling and pushing and shoving.

"Courtney," she whispered with all the calm she could muster, "move with me toward the shelves."

"Courtney," Ellis crooned. "Baby, we've got such a good thing going. Do you honestly think I'd do anything to hurt you?" He was sweet-talking her now and stood with his hands held innocently at his sides. "Or our baby?"

His syrupy words stopped Courtney, and Kendall bumped into her. "Don't listen to him." She gave Courtney a gently nudge. To her relief, Courtney continued toward the ammunition just a few feet away. "Open the gun."

Ellis took several steps toward them. Kendall swung the ax in a threatening gesture, and he stopped.

"I can't do it," Courtney cried.

"Yes, you can." Kendall couldn't let Courtney fall apart on her now. "Just push the lever on top to one side, then push down on the barrel." From the corner of her eye, she saw Courtney fumbling with the gun.

"I have it. Now what do I do?"

Kendall inclined her head toward the shells. "Load it. The red shells, I think——"

Ellis laughed, a loud and frightening sound that put goose bumps on Kendall's arms. "You don't really think I'm going to stand here and let you load that gun, do you?"

Distracted by his angry voice, Kendall wasn't prepared for his assault. He lunged forward, his body slamming into Kendall full force. She couldn't breathe for several long seconds, but the sound of Courtney's screaming forced her into action.

All she could see was Ellis astraddle Courtney, swearing and pounding her head against the floor. A protective instinct as old as time surged to life inside Kendall, and she scrambled across the floor to knock him off her sister. She barely had time to pick herself up before he was upon her, striking her across the face.

She staggered backward from the force of the blow, and Ellis attacked again. He shoved her against the wall, pinning her with his body and one forearm across her throat. His strength surprised her. Strong though she was, she was no match for him.

"I should have known you'd be more trouble than you were worth back in Houston," he snarled, his face inches from hers. He had to take time to catch his breath. "You're in better shape than I remembered." With a glance over his shoulder at Courtney's unconscious form, he pressed his lower body intimately closer. "She's not a bad lover, you know." His eyes were glassy now, his voice low and breathy. "But she's not you." He moved his arm from her throat, let his hand slide down the front of her shirt.

She'd lain in this man's bed before, dreamed of being his wife, but after Jake, his touch sickened her—*he* was sick. With strength that surprised them both, she struggled against him, tried to bring her knee up. He anticipated the move and pressed her harder against the wall. Afraid that her ribs would crack from the pressure, she screamed and watched him draw back his fist.

The blow never landed; she opened her eyes to see Jake dragging Ellis off her. She'd never seen Jake lose control before, and it was a frightening sight. He swore and slammed Ellis against the same wall he'd had her pinned to. Ellis never knew what hit him and slumped in an unconscious heap on the floor.

Jake towered above him, his fingers flexing into tight fists, his chest heaving. "Damn. I wasn't finished with him." Kendall heard the need for retribution in his voice and was glad that Ellis had gone down so easily. They didn't need the complication of a charge of police brutality.

"Is she okay?" Jake asked, nodding toward Courtney as he cuffed Ellis's hands behind him, rendering the lowlife totally powerless.

Kendall had been so startled to see Jake that she, too, seemed in a stupor. Quickly moving to Courtney's side, she was relieved to find her coming around. She helped Courtney to a chair, then faced Jake.

He stood across the room, a short distance of no more than twenty feet that seemed to her like miles.

Now that the danger had passed, she felt tremors building inside her. "I'm sorry," she heard herself whisper.

That's all it took to get him across the room. "Sorry? For what?" His arms around her had never felt so comforting or safe.

Tears stung her eyes. "This is supposed to be our special place, and I brought Courtney and Ellis here." She heard him chuckle as he pulled her closer.

"Then we won't remember that." He glanced at

Courtney sitting dazed in a chair, then at Ellis unconscious on the floor. He raised his hand to gently caress Kendall's cheek. "Or that your face was red and swollen when I officially asked you to be my wife." He took her in his arms and kissed her. She kissed him back, not caring that it hurt just to breathe.

"I'll take that as a yes," he said, smiling. "Aren't you going to ask me how the meeting went?"

"Yes, of course, I am."

"It's settled. The board thanked Mrs. Tyler and Marianne for their concern but agreed with my position that as long as I do my job and the program is successful, my personal life has nothing to do with funding."

"How did Mrs. Tyler take it?"

"She gave a very unladylike snort, then left in a huff." He had the most adorable grin. "But not before I invited her and everyone else there to the wedding."

"You didn't?"

"I did."

Kendall felt like laughing, so she did. "I love you."

"I know." He gave her a quick peck. "Now help me get these two on their feet. We still have some celebrating to do."

She stopped him with a touch on his arm. "What about Courtney?"

Jake's expression sobered. "I'll do everything I can to help her, but she has to be willing to help herself."

"Will she have to go to jail today?"

"I think I can work around that. She's welcome to stay at the house." He cupped her chin. "In your room until the new housekeeper gets settled in."

"New housekeeper? Jake, what have you done?"

"Something completely and totally selfish." He leaned down to whisper against her lips, "Just making sure you have plenty of time to cherish me back."

_____ EPILOGUE _____

"He said to send you right in when you got here, Mrs. Sentell."

Kendall thanked Stephanie and eased the door open. Inside, Jake's voice sounded cool, efficient, and authoritative.

"Ex-cons, parolees, and probationers need all the help they can get reentering society. Being able to find work usually decides whether or not they make it. Our success rate's been remarkable, and I see no reason that you won't fit right in." He looked up and smiled. "We're almost finished."

Even after a year of marriage, her reaction to something as innocent as his smile still surprised Kendall. She returned his smile, then winked at Courtney.

Taking a seat, she remembered the day she had sat exactly where Courtney was sitting and listened to the same speech. She let her gaze drift away from Jake to linger on the photo sitting on the credenza behind his desk. The photographer had done an excellent job capturing the love in the Sentell family. Brad, Josh,

Timmy, and Matt stood proud and tall behind Jake and herself while Becca smiled impishly from her perch in her father's lap. A larger copy of the portrait hung in Jake's study at home, replacing the one he'd given to Becky's parents.

"I shouldn't have to tell you that contact with certain people from your past is strictly forbidden, so I won't," she heard Jake saying. Some things never changed. It was the same warning he'd issued her over a year ago. "The owners of Red Apple Nursery School are excited about being able to contribute to the reentry program, and just as I promised, you'll be able to keep Leigh with you."

Courtney gave him a grateful smile and looked at Kendall, who had taken the baby out of her carry seat. "I don't know what I'd have done without your help. I won't let you down."

"Just don't let your baby down," Jake said, taking Leigh from her aunt. "Now you three go on and have a good day shopping. I have work to do." He tweaked the baby's nose then gave her back to her mother.

"Go ahead, Courtney," Kendall said. "I'll catch up."

Once Courtney closed the door, Jake turned Kendall into his waiting arms. "I thought they'd never leave." His kiss stole her breath away. "You know, you looked real natural holding Leigh like that. Sure you don't want us to have one of our own?"

Kendall hugged him tighter around the waist. "Don't you think we have enough children to worry about? Besides, it won't be long before Brad thinks about marriage and starting his own family. With the way the Sentell men reproduce, we'll probably have more babies than we'll know what to do with, Grandpa."

"Ouch, that smarts."

Kendall couldn't help laughing. "That's what you get for becoming a father so young." She kissed him on the chin. "Besides, if it happens for us, it happens. If it doesn't, no big deal." And it was true. She had everything she'd ever wanted. Jake made each day an exciting new adventure; the boys loved her for who she was and for making their father happy; Becca had started calling her Mommy shortly after the wedding; and Courtney was going to be okay, thanks to Jake.

"I like the way you think."

"You keep telling me that."

His gray eyes twinkled mischievously. "You keep thinking the way I like."

"This sounds like a conversation that's going nowhere."

"You're probably right, but I like going nowhere with you."

Kendall raised one eyebrow. "Jacob Heath Sentell, you're starting to worry me."

"Sorry," he said, but she could see that he was anything but. "Guess things are going too smoothly around here. Let's stir up some trouble. Wanna go skinny-dippin'?"

"Jake . . ."

"Okay," he said, feigning disappointment. "Let's drop Courtney off at her place and go up to the cabin and—"

"Do something special?"

He raised his hand to gently caress her cheek. "I *do* like the way you think."

He could drive her crazy with the most innocent touch. Crazy in the nicest sense of the word.

"You keep telling me that."

He lowered his head to hers. "You keep thinking the way I like."

"Here we go again," she whispered against his nibbling lips.

"And again and again and again." His voice was low and seductive and so very sexy. "If we're very, very lucky."

SHARE THE FUN . . .
SHARE YOUR NEW-FOUND TREASURE!!

You don't want to let your new books out of your sight? That's okay. Your friends can get their own. Order below.

No. 136 HIGH-RIDING HEROES by Joey Light
Victoria was going to stand her ground whether Wes liked it or not!

No. 137 HOMEWARD BOUND by Kathryn Attalla
Jake resented Kate's sudden intrusion into his quiet, settled life.

No. 138 NO ILLUSION by Lynnette Kent
When Chloe meets Peter, she finds magic does not make life any simpler.

No. 140 LOVE IN BLOOM by Karen Rose Smith
Clay has no past that he can remember. Can he make a future with Paige?

No. 141 BEDROOM EYES by Becky Barker
Nate solves Liana's dilemma but he causes a whole new set of problems.

No. 142 LIFESAVER by Janice Bartlett
Megan had no choice but to save Mac's life but now she's in danger, too.

No. 143 HEAVENLY by Carol Bogolin
Men like David were the ultimate temptation and Kathlyn vowed to resist!

No. 144 OUTSIDE THE RULES by Linda Hughes
Jamie and Stephen play a dangerous game with high stakes and no rules.
